LIFE'S FOREVER CHANGED
PREQUEL to the SHOW ME SERIES
Published by Anne Stone

Copyright ©2017 Judith A Seligstein Living Trust
978-0-9970691-9-8

This is a work of fiction. Names, characters, places and incidents are either the product of the author's imagination or are used fictitiously, and any resemblance to actual persons, living or dead, business establishments, events or locales is entirely coincidental.

Printed in the USA.

Editing, Cover Design and Interior Format

Life's

FOREVER
CHANGED

The Show Me Series

THE PREQUEL

Anne Stone

To Baba, there isn't a day that doesn't go by that I don't think of you! To my sister, Isabel—thanks for being my sounding board. And as always, to you Dad. I wouldn't be on this journey without your encouragement.

Prologue

ॐ

IT WAS A WARM SUMMER day in St. Louis—hotter than all get out, the last day before Alejandro left for the University of Wisconsin. He'd procrastinated all summer with this visit, but he needed to accomplish it before heading home for his going away party. It was one of the hardest things he'd done in a long, long time.

He made a left turn and entered the one place he had avoided for more than two years. The vivid green grass surprised him as he came to the fork in the road. After a long, hot summer, most everything was brown, but not here. The fresh growth made him feel a bit brighter as he made his journey. He wound his way through the various roads, all the while hoping he wouldn't get lost. He'd been here only the one time, and he recalled that winter day in vivid detail. It had been bitter cold. He remembered walking into church for the funeral mass beside his mother and friends and then driving the lonely miles that led to him saying a final goodbye to his best friend. Today as he drove along, he shivered, recalling the bitter wind as it had whipped through the pin oak trees, rattling the last of the leaves that still hung on their branches as he rounded the bend that led to Jacob.

Jacob and he had become best friends in kindergarten and had experienced everything together from learning how to tie their shoes to the big day when they crossed over from Cub Scouts to Boy Scouts. They'd even held a joint Court of Honor when they received their Eagle Scout Awards. They were like two peas in a pod. Wherever Jacob was, Alejandro wasn't far behind, and vice versa.

Alejandro slowed the car as he approached the section he'd committed to memory— section fifteen. He remembered the number because they were both fifteen when he'd lost his friend.

As he eased his car along, he searched for the marker that signified where Jacob lay. This was an older section to the cemetery and held intricately carved monuments made from granite. And then he saw the one that was shaped like the George Washington Memorial and was surrounded by four granite carved chairs. As soon as he saw that, he knew he wasn't far.

Alejandro pulled to the side of the road and parked. He exited the car and took in his surroundings. It was peaceful as he breathed in the warm air. He strolled up the uneven stone steps laid into the hillside. Jacob's grave overlooked the cemetery on one side and the Missouri River on the other.

It took him a few moments to discover the stone. Someone had recently left a bunch of flowers and they still retained a bit of freshness to them. He read Jacob's name. Both the birthday and date of death were inscribed into Alejandro's memory, days he'd never forget.

Jacob had been ill, and it took his doctors too long to diagnose his illness. By the time they discovered it, his kidneys were barely functioning. He'd been placed on dialysis that helped some, but in the end, he'd died before he could have a kidney transplant. And on that day, when Alejandro forever lost his friend, he made a solemn vow. Instead of following in his father's footsteps into pediatric medicine, he made a decision that would forever change his life. Alejandro Alvarez would become a nephrologist and then focus on becoming a transplant surgeon. He wanted to save as many lives as he could because he wasn't able to save Jacob's.

Alejandro ran his hand along Jacob's name. "I've never forgotten you, my friend. You are always with me." As he spoke, a cardinal landed on the adjacent tombstone. It sat there listening to him as he spoke. "I'm heading off to college tomorrow, and I don't know when I'll be back again. You remember how I was going to follow my dad into his practice? Well, I'm not. I'm going to help people that are afflicted with the same disease you had. If I can save just one life, I'll be happy because I would do anything to have saved yours. I miss you more than words can say. We experienced all of our firsts together, and life hasn't been the same without you in it." The bird squawked at him. He took one look at it and contemplated if Jacob was listening to him.

"I'm going to make a difference, Jacob. I'm sorry it's taken me so long to come by and see you, but I didn't have it in me. I'll always remember our times together, and I hope to see you on the other side."

Alejandro took one last look at the monument and turned back to his car. The squawking bird flew right in front of him, causing him to stop abruptly. The bird landed on a tree limb right beside his car. A sense of calm came over him as he took one last glance at the monument. "Goodbye, my friend," he said as he opened his car door. The bird called out one last time as it circled his car and returned in the direction of Jacob's grave.

Alejandro closed the car door. Life as he knew it was coming to an end, and he wasn't going to look back. He'd miss his family tremendously. He knew he would no longer have the freedom to come and go as he pleased. Medical school was going to be tough, and it would now become his sole focus. He'd do anything in his power to make a difference and forever change people's lives.

Chapter One

Fourteen years later...

IT WAS JUST AFTER TWO in the morning. For the first time in hours, Alejandro had been able to sit, if only for a few moments. Closing his eyes, he revisited his day. It began with the news that a heart had become available for a precious little boy, a six-month-old infant. He'd spent a good deal of his day in surgery and then spent hours monitoring Frederick in recovery.

He ran his fingers through his hair and glanced down at the hands on his watch. That's when he noticed the date. Today would have been Jacob's birthday. So much had changed in his life and yet much had remained the same. His career choices had altered somewhat over the years. He'd completed his studies in nephrology, then he'd become a transplant surgeon and never once looked back as it allowed him to use his skills in more ways than he'd ever dreamed possible. He knew his friend would be thrilled with all of his accomplishments; unfortunately, they ultimately resulted from Jacob's death.

As he sat contemplating his life, Alejandro realized that the niggling feeling he'd carried with him lately had resurfaced. On top of missing his best friend, he acknowledged how lonely he felt. By now, he thought, both he and Jacob would have been married with children. Thinking of his parents and siblings, he knew he needed to take some time off and return to St. Louis. It had been quite a while since he'd seen his family. He missed them dearly, but mostly he missed his sister Gabriella. She was the youngest of his siblings, and while growing up, he'd always been there for her before he graduated high school. He'd left for college right before she turned eleven and hadn't been home much since. He'd lost out on so much of her life. Medical school and then his residencies were his focus, and he'd barely given his family much thought until recently. He'd stayed in touch and traveled home, but not as often as he should have. Now he realized what the nagging feeling stemmed from. He'd been alone too long, and he needed to find someone to share his life with.

After watching baby Fredrick's struggles during surgery, he'd finally come to the conclusion that he wanted—no, needed—someone in his life. Someone that he could go home to and share his day with. Share both his successes and failures. Someone that he could wrap in his arms, who would listen to him and understand his daily triumphs and the disappointments that affected him more than he even realized. The losses stayed with him and were never forgotten. Often times, he'd analyzed where he'd gone wrong, coming to the conclusion that nothing he'd done would have saved his patient.

He rubbed the back of his neck and thought of Frederick. He'd been surprised when he saw one of the nurses from the Pediatric Intensive Care Unit in the hallway outside of Recovery. He'd worked with Tammy Johansen closely over the last several months. He knew she was a devoted nurse to her patients. He hadn't spoken to her but did overhear her asking about Frederick. When the recovery nurse informed her of his condition, a bright smile broke out across her face, and then she moved on, presumably back to her unit.

As he sat in his office, he knew he needed to make changes in his life. He'd been going non-stop for months on end, and he needed to slow down before the long hours caught up with him. He was having a hard time rebounding after a long day. He should step away before he made a mistake. As soon as his schedule allowed, he decided, he'd take a few days off.

Alejandro had been up all night, outside of taking a brief break; he'd spent the majority of it in Recovery with Frederick. It had been touch and go, but the child seemed to be out of danger. As he entered the Pediatric ICU, he ran his hand along his forehead. Losing sight of where he was, he ran smack into Tammy, who was assigned to Frederick's care. "Sorry about that." He ran his hand through his already disheveled hair. "It's been quite a night. I think he has finally stabilized."

He was fully aware of Tammy's concern about baby Frederick, especially after her visit to the Recovery Unit and wasn't surprised that she hadn't gone home herself. "Thanks for staying. I'm sure it helped his parents, knowing you were here."

"I couldn't leave." She shook her head. "That little guy's been through so much since he was born. I was here that night, too, when he was rushed into the NICU. I was covering for a friend that had called in sick."

"Let's keep our fingers crossed." Alejandro tried to contain a yawn, but somehow it slipped out. "I need a coffee. Care to join me? I'm buying."

"That sounds really good right about now."

Alejandro was glad she accepted his invitation. She was single, and after his earlier thoughts of family, he decided he wanted to get to know her. What a better opportunity, especially with what they'd gone through in the last twenty-four hours.

While they waited for the elevator, she leaned against the wall as if it kept her upright. "Maybe you should go home. You look really tired," he said.

"Nah, I'll be fine. Give me that cup of coffee, and I'll bounce right back. It's not like I haven't been down this road before. Sometimes these little guys get under my skin, and I can't help that I want to see their care through."

Just then, the elevator arrived. They were alone as they rode down to the lower level where the cafeteria was located. Luscious smells greeted them as the doors opened. "I think I need to change my order from just coffee to a full-out breakfast. All of a sudden I'm starved, what about you?"

"I could eat too." They went through the line where they both selected fruit, eggs and toast.

"Don't forget your coffee," he called over his shoulder as he added creamer to his.

"Never. It's going to be my kryptonite today." He waited while she poured her coffee and then stood behind her in line. He motioned to Crystal, the cashier, that he was paying for both of their breakfasts.

She surprisingly smiled back at him.

Alejandro led Tammy to a back corner of the cafeteria. He held her chair as she sat and then returned their trays to the dishwasher.

He knew the basics about Tammy— that was about it. "So tell me a little about yourself. I know you graduated from the UW. Are you from the area?"

"I am. I grew up just outside of Madison. My parents still live here, but my siblings have both moved on. My brother, Maximus, lives in Lancaster, PA and my sister, Elsa, lives in the Upper Peninsula. What about you?"

"I'm originally from St. Louis, but I moved here to go to school and haven't left since."

"Do you get home often?"

"On rare occasions, definitely not as often as I should." He sipped his coffee. "Have you always worked in pediatrics?"

"I have."

"Did you work at another hospital? I don't remember you roaming the halls until recently."

"About that…I started here after I graduated from nursing school but returned after a short stay at another hospital. I missed the camaraderie here. I went to school with many of my peers and, in fact, some of my professors still walk these halls. You know the old adage: the grass is always greener on the other side? Well that's definitely not true for me." She traced the edge of her coffee cup as if contemplating her next thoughts. "I returned about a year ago. In fact, I worked with you on my very first day back."

He wasn't exactly sure when that happened because all he remembered was she appeared out of nowhere. He'd acknowledged her presence almost immediately but never questioned where she'd come from. But now, he was overjoyed with where his mind was taking him.

They'd spent more time chatting when he glanced at his watch. "We'd better get back." They gathered their trash and headed down the long hallway that led to the elevators. As they neared them, he decided now was the best time to ask the question that had filled his thoughts since they first sat down to eat, "I enjoyed this." Smiling at her he asked, "Would you like to go out sometime?"

She thought for the briefest of moments. Smiling broadly at him, she answered, "Yeah, I would."

"I'd suggest tonight, but we know why that wouldn't work."

"No, I'd probably fall asleep in my food."

"Me too. I know when my shift ends, I'll be ready to face plant it myself. I'm off this weekend, what about you?"

"I am, as well."

"Are you free Saturday evening?"

She didn't have to think twice. "I am free and I'd love to go out with you."

"Let's make it a date then." Alejandro escorted her back to the PICU. He pulled out his phone. "What's your number?" She rattled it off to him, and he immediately dialed it. Pointing at his phone, he said, "Now I've got it in my cell, and you also have mine. Text me your address." He grinned then headed off to his office. His schedule was full for the day with back-to-back appointments, and he wouldn't return to the unit until later. As he walked along, he realized his day had started off pretty well. Frederick was holding his own, and Tammy had agreed to go out with him.

Alejandro checked his phone several times throughout the day, but there was no text from Tammy. By the time he made his way back to the PICU, she'd already left. As he drove home, his phone chimed with an incoming text. At the first chance, he checked it. She'd sent him her address along with a message. *"I can't wait until Saturday. See you then."*

Friday dragged on for Alejandro. He had one crisis after another and missed seeing Tammy's bright and shining face when he visited the PICU. He texted that night. *Sorry our paths didn't cross today. I was looking forward to seeing you. I can't wait until our date tomorrow. Until then…*

He felt good after sending his message. He hadn't dated much since leaving St. Louis and was looking forward to their night out. His focus had been on getting through medical school and his residencies. Now he felt the freedom to date as long as he could fit it into his busy schedule. He thought for a minute and decided. *I'm not going to fit it into my schedule. I'm going to make the time.* Alejandro had recently turned thirty-two and he'd like to start a family. He didn't want to be too old to enjoy his children. Now that he was somewhat settled with his career, he knew it was time to put down roots and find the woman of his dreams. As he drove along, he contemplated if Tammy could be that woman.

Saturday dragged on for Alejandro. He couldn't contain himself any longer and arrived at her home almost twenty minutes early after stopping off at a nearby florist where he chose a lovely bouquet of mixed flowers. He wanted to set the stage on a night that he imagined would forever change his life.

He hoped that she'd be ready and almost talked

himself out of knocking on the door earlier than she expected. He decided to give it a try. What's the worst that could happen? She wouldn't be dressed? He apprehensively rang the doorbell. He was surprised when she answered quickly. Her face lit up when she realized it was him. "Sorry I'm a bit early. I couldn't wait a minute longer to see you." She moved aside so he could enter.

"Here, these are for you." He presented her with the bouquet as he crossed the threshold. The surprised look on her face said it all. He'd done the right thing with his spur-of-the-moment decision. Flowers definitely were the way to go. Turning, he really looked at her. She took his breath away. "Wow, you look beautiful."

"Oh my! These are gorgeous and smell wonderful. Let me put them in some water."

He followed her as she made her way to the kitchen, grabbing a vase from an open shelf. He could tell she was pleased with his gesture as she smiled the entire time she added water to the vase.

Fingering the petals of one of the flowers, she said, "Thank you, but you didn't have to buy me flowers." Shyly she looked up at him. "I have the perfect spot for them." She reached for the vase and made her way into the foyer where a plant stand stood beside her door. "Perfect," she added as she set them down. "The smell will permeate the air, and I'll be able to see them from the family room." She reached in and brushed a kiss against his cheek. "Thanks," she quietly said as she reached for her coat. "So, where are we going?" she asked as he helped her on with it.

"I made reservations for Sterling's."

"Oh my, I haven't been there in forever. It's so fancy,

and popular."

"For their fish fries, maybe."

"Yeah, I guess you're right. I haven't been there for anything else, so this will definitely be a treat for me."

"We'll see what it's like then. I've only been there for Happy Hour and, of course, their infamous fish fry." He placed his arm about her waist and guided her to the car. He held the door as she sat down on the leather seat. The bottom of her dress was sticking out of the car and he reached down to sweep it back inside.

"Thanks, I didn't notice my dress." He shut the car door and walked around to the driver's side. She was more beautiful than he realized since he'd only seen her in scrubs and no make-up at the hospital. He hoped their evening together was the beginning of something special.

He slid into the car and started the engine. He placed his arm against the back of her seat and turned to her. "I have to say, you look absolutely stunning tonight. Your scrubs definitely don't do you justice."

"Are they supposed to?" She chuckled.

"No, I guess they're not." With that he put the car in drive and headed in the direction of Sterling's.

He had already decided to use the valet service and was glad that he did, for as he pulled up to the restaurant, the parking lot was packed. He jumped out of the car, reaching Tammy's door before the valet. Alejandro extended his hand and helped her from the car wrapping her hand securely in his. He grabbed his claim check and barely heard the valet wish him a good evening.

They were early for their reservation, so they made their way into the bar where he ordered them each a glass of wine. "I can't believe how crowded it is," she claimed as she sipped her wine.

He laughed, "I think everyone's spending their evening here." It was relatively loud in the bar, so he leaned into her as he spoke. "It is a Saturday night." He watched her nod as she looked around. "Maybe I should have chosen something less crowded for our first date."

"Eh, don't worry about it." She paused and looked at the television overhead. "Didn't the Badgers have a home game today? You know how crazy this town gets when there's a game."

"I think you're right. I wonder if they won."

A couple sitting next to them chimed in. "They won! When don't they?"

"You've got a point there. They've had a stellar season so far," Alejandro said. "I bet they'll be in the Rose Bowl again this year."

Just as he was about to comment further, they were called for their table. He placed his hand along her back as they wound their way through the restaurant and up the stairs to the second floor. Almost immediately, he noticed a change in the atmosphere. It was certainly less noisy as he held her chair while she sat down. *Maybe it wasn't such a bad choice.*

Their evening flew by. They discussed little Frederick and his prognosis, and he shared with her his love of fishing.

"I was never so happy to see the little one get his new heart," Tammy said as she sipped her wine.

"We were lucky there. I'm not sure how much longer he would have hung on."

"I wasn't aware that he was that critical."

A glass dropped with a loud crash against the floor causing him to temporarily lose his focus. He was ready to reply when their entrees were served. She'd ordered a chicken breast stuffed with Gruyere cheese, apples, and cranberries, and he ordered boneless beef short ribs braised in beer.

As they ate, she asked, "So what do you like to do in your spare time?"

"I love to fish. It's so peaceful sitting alone in the quiet solitude. I get a lot of thinking done while fishing."

"I guess that's a good thing, right?"

"It can be, but then there are times when I can't seem to turn off my thoughts, and my planned day to unwind falls apart."

"I hope that doesn't happen too often."

"It doesn't, not really. Usually, it's after a particularly difficult case, and I ponder what I could have done better." He took another bite of his short ribs and then asked, "What about you? What do you like to do?"

"Crafts. I'm all about crafts from painting to knitting to scrapbooking. I do it all. In fact, I often drive up to Stevens Point and visit one of the big craft retailers. I love to go in June when they have their warehouse sale. If you're a crafter, it's definitely something you should do."

Pointing to himself, he said, "I'm not a crafter, but I'd go along just so I could spend the day with you."

She leaned her elbow on the table and rested her chin on her palm and smiled at him. "I think you'd be bored stiff."

"Maybe, maybe not, but I guess we won't know if I don't give it a try."

"Well, mark your calendar for mid-June. The sale's always held the week of Father's Day."

"Done. I'll put it on the calendar."

He enjoyed the rest of their evening, and before he knew it, he was once again pulling into her driveway. He turned off the ignition and turned to her. "I had a really nice time tonight." He glanced into her sparkling blue eyes. He hoped she felt the same way. He reached over and slid his hand along the side of her face. "What about you?"

"Once we got past the noise of the bar, and I could hear what you were saying," she laughed. "Yeah, I had a good time. Better than good. Fabulous, I might add."

"So did I." He began to play with her hair, winding a few tendrils around his finger. "So—"

"So?"

"Will you go out with me again?" She nodded. He didn't want to be too assuming, but he didn't think, only spoke. "How about tomorrow?" She giggled. "Is that too soon for you?"

She reached up and wrapped her fingers around his hand that was laced in her hair. "I would love to go out with you tomorrow."

Smiling broadly, he said, "It's supposed to be a nice day. Let's go for a drive up north."

"I'd like that." And then he leaned across the seat and brushed his lips against hers. She seemed surprised at first but then went with the kiss. As he pulled away, he realized how soft her lips were.

"I hope I wasn't being too forward."

"No, you weren't. In fact, I really liked it."

"Well then," he spoke as he reached for her and pulled her into his arms, kissing her once again.

All too soon, their kiss ended and he reached for his door. "I don't want to move too fast here. We can pick this up again tomorrow." He knew he surprised her with his kiss and imagined that she was trying to wrap her mind around what he'd said to her when he opened her car door.

Their evening had come to an end much too quickly. He'd waited for what seemed like an eternity for their date to begin, and in the blink of an eye, he'd found himself returning her home. "Until tomorrow." He leaned in and dropped a kiss to her cheek.

"Tomorrow," she practically whispered as he walked back to his car. As he started to drive away, he noticed her brush her fingertips along her cheek. A huge smile had broken out on her face as she waved good-bye. *Where has she been all of my life? Until tomorrow,* he thought as he drove home to his lonely apartment. As he walked through the door, he looked around. *Maybe this place won't be too lonely much longer.* He wasn't exactly tired as his mind was racing. He grabbed a beer and the television remote. He mindlessly sat roving through the cable channels, doing his best not to think about their evening. Tammy's smile was the last thing he thought of as he drifted off to sleep.

Chapter Two

TAMMY HAD A HARDER THAN normal time rising Monday morning. She and Alejandro had spent a good part of Sunday up in the Dells. They took a scenic drive from Madison and ended up at the Indian casino where they each were a little richer when they left.

As they drove along the winding country road that ran along the water, they came across a quaint restaurant that overlooked the Wisconsin River. It was late afternoon when he pulled into the parking lot. With no cars in sight, they weren't sure if it was open until they saw the brightly lit sign.

She met him at the edge of the sidewalk where he grabbed ahold of her hand. "I guess they're open," she commented as she squeezed his fingers.

Pointing, he said, "The open sign's on and calling us." He was a tad surprised when he tugged on the door and it swung out. He'd really thought they'd forgotten to turn off the sign from the previous day. Placing his hand on her lower back, he guided her into the dimly lit room. He was surprised when they were greeted by a friendly older gentleman.

"Welcome to Frieda's. Any particular spot you'd like to sit?" he asked as he gestured to the empty restaurant.

"How about the deck?" she replied.

"Miss, good choice," the man said. "It's the perfect night for that." He guided them outside. "Something to drink?" They both requested iced teas. "Be right back with your drinks. By the way, my name's Sam. I'm the owner, host, and your waiter tonight."

"Are you all alone?" Tammy inquired.

"Nah, Jonesy, my cook, is here. We normally don't open until five on a Sunday, but I decided to light the sign a little early. I guess today's your lucky day."

"I believe you're right." Alejandro reached for Tammy's hand.

As they sipped their iced teas and waited on their dinner, out of nowhere Alejandro asked, "How come the PICU?"

He watched the emotions cross her face, and then she shared with him the reason why she'd chosen to work there. Her sister, Elsa, had been born prematurely. Not only did she spend an inordinate amount of time in the Neonatal Intensive Care Unit but also had been hospitalized on several occasions in the PICU.

"I wanted to give back something," Tammy said. "My parents still speak about their experiences when Elsa was hospitalized, and all these years later my mom continues to rave about a nurse that meant the world to her. When I decided to become a nurse, I wanted to be someone that my patients remembered, that made a difference while they endured a traumatic time in their lives. If I can ease the pain for just one family making their stay a little bit less stressful, I've done my job."

As he listened to her, he fell more under her spell. She was a special woman that practically came out of nowhere. He felt like he'd been struck by lightning, causing him to open his eyes a little wider. She'd been right in front of his face all along, and all it took was that one brief moment in time to change the course of his trajectory.

Their meal was outstanding, one he knew he'd always remember. She'd shared with him a memory that he was sure still influenced her family to this day. It meant a great deal to him that she felt comfortable enough to share her sister's story.

By the time he arrived at her home, it was close to eleven. They'd decided on an after-dinner drink and listened as a piano player played romantic ballads from the seventies and eighties. There'd been a small dance floor that he wooed her onto. He pulled her into his arms, holding her closely as they swayed to the sounds of the piano. It was a magical time for him, holding her in his arms. As the last song ended, he brushed a kiss against her forehead. He realized the time and knew she worked the early shift and needed to get home to sleep.

Tammy woke up at five. She rose early so she could walk before heading into the hospital. That insured that she got in her daily exercise. If she waited until she returned home, she was often spent and didn't have the drive to hop on the treadmill.

She arrived at the hospital later than normal. Usually she got there at least a half hour before her shift began, but today, she barely made it before it started. As she entered the PICU, her glance immediately found Alejandro. He was seated behind a desk, entering data into a patient's chart. He looked tired. She wondered if he'd gotten any sleep.

Several of her peers stood around the main desk. She didn't want to draw attention to him, so she went about getting ready for the day. Over dinner the night before, they decided to keep their relationship just between the two of them for the time being. Neither wanted to hear the gossip about their dating running rampant around the hospital.

She was reading a memorandum when she felt him approach. She glanced up and caught his half-smile. "Morning," he breathed as he raised his hand to his forehead swiping his fingers through his hair.

"Are you just arriving or have you been here all night?"

He leaned closer towards her so no one could hear their conversation. "I got a call right after I left your house."

"Is it Frederick?" She caught the expression of concern cross his face.

"Yeah." He took a deep breath and sighed. "He's okay right now. It's been a long night for his parents. Try and keep an eye on them today. They're walking zombies right about now."

"Sure, anything you need." His eyes scanned the area before his hand reached for hers. She had assumed he didn't want anyone watching their interaction, but he leaned toward her. She wasn't sure what he was up to.

"I had a really nice time yesterday." She thought she heard someone approaching and spun her head in the direction of the noise. No one was there. She guessed her imagination was playing tricks on her.

"Will you meet me for lunch? I have a consultation late this morning, and then I'm free for the remainder of the day."

"Maybe you can get some sleep."

"Maybe." He squeezed her hand. "You didn't answer my question. Will you come to my office for lunch? I'll order in."

"I'd like that," she whispered as she noticed a maintenance person walk by.

He pulled away and winked. "I'll see you at one?"

"I'll be there."

❧

They had a nice lunch. He'd ordered from a deli located around the corner from the hospital. He had the beginnings of a headache and knew how noisy the cafeteria was this time of day. He also didn't want them to be seen together, especially with how new their relationship was. He was almost certain she'd enjoy it being just the two of them. They could talk and avoid being interrupted.

"So much for the peace and quiet of my office," he said as he hung up the phone for the umpteenth time. "I certainly thought we wouldn't be disturbed here."

"Don't worry about it, Alejandro." She looked at the clock on his wall. "I've got to go."

"Are you up for dinner tonight?"

"Three evenings in a row?"

He bowed his head and leaned in closer again. "I thought I'd ask."

"And I'm glad you did. Why don't you come over to my house and I'll cook. We can relax and enjoy just ourselves without being interrupted."

"I like that idea."

"I'd better get going." She crumpled up her wrapper and threw it away. She stood and walked over to him. Leaning over, she placed a gentle kiss on his lips. "Get some rest. I'll see you at six?"

"Sure thing." He reached for her hand and pulled her towards him. Wrapping his arms around her waist, he placed his head on her shoulder. "I'm going to miss you." He tightened his hold. "Until this evening." He reached up and kissed her soft lips and let her go.

He watched her stroll to the door. Turning back to him, she said, "Thanks for lunch." Then she disappeared through the door.

He hadn't realized he'd been holding his breath until he released it. He recognized that for the first time in his life, he could see a future with a woman. All through school, he'd gone out with women but only as friends. He'd never been involved in a serious relationship. He now considered what he had with Tammy as potentially serious. They'd spent a good part of the weekend together and he was beginning to believe he could spend the rest of his life with her. He wondered *am I moving too quickly here? Should I slow down?*

His thoughts were all over the place. He decided he'd approach her tonight. Determine what she was thinking and feeling herself. He hoped he wasn't mistaken and that this wasn't one-sided.

Alejandro dozed off and was awakened by his ringing cell. He glanced at the caller and discovered it was his sister. "Hey, Gabby, what's up?"

"Just checking in. I haven't heard from you in a few days. If fact, I thought I'd get your voicemail. I'm surprised you answered."

"I have the afternoon off. What's new in the Lou?"

"Not much. We're on fall break next week. I was wondering if you'll be around. I thought maybe I'd drive up and see my big brother for a few days. I haven't seen you in *forever*." She heard him sigh. "It's okay if you're busy. Maybe next time."

He heard the disappointment in her voice. "No, it's not that. I'd love to see you. Can you come up on Tuesday? I'm off next Wednesday so we can hang out."

"You're sure? Alejandro, I miss you, and I'd really like to spend some time with you— Tuesday would be perfect." He knew she was excited and did not want to disappoint her. Depending on how he and Tammy were getting along, maybe he'd introduce them.

"I've got another call coming in. Call me later in the week, and we'll make plans, okay?"

"Sure thing. Oh, and Mom says hi too." He smiled when he heard her last comment. He knew what she was implying. He hadn't phoned home in over a week and guessed he'd better call his mother before the day was over.

Whoever was calling on the other line had hung up by the time he got off with Gabriella. He had a minute and immediately phoned his mother. "Hi, Mom," he said when she answered.

"Son, how are you? It's been a while since you phoned."

"I feel like I've been burning the midnight oil for the last two weeks. It's been one crisis after another." They talked for a few minutes and then she put John on the phone. "Hi, Dad. What are you doing home? Today's not your day off."

"I was feeling a little under the weather and didn't want to expose anyone. Alec and Joe can take care of everything." His brothers were both pediatricians and worked alongside their father at the practice he'd opened thirty years ago.

"I'm sure they can." He listened as his father went on about a virus that was running rampant in St. Louis.

"Yeah, I've heard there's one going around here too." He heard his phone buzz. "Hey Dad, I've got to go. I have another call coming in."

"Sure thing, son. We'll talk soon."

This time Alejandro was able to get to the call before the caller hung up. He wished he'd let it go to voice-mail since this time it was a wrong number.

He checked his watch. He needed to hurry home if he was going to shower before picking up flowers and a bottle of wine for their dinner. He knew how much she enjoyed her bouquet from the other night and decided to surprise her with another. Maybe roses this time. He made it home in fifteen minutes and, after a quick shower, felt renewed. Since they were staying in, he threw on a pair of jeans and a sweater.

Promptly at six he walked up her sidewalk. He felt a spring to his step that he hadn't experienced in a long time. He was anxious to see her and wasn't dis-appointed when she opened the door. She'd dressed casually in jeans and a Wisconsin Badger sweatshirt. Her eyes were glowing as he stepped inside her door. She was just as happy to see him as he was her. Leaning in, he brushed her cheek with a kiss, then, produced the bouquet of roses and bottle of wine.

"Oh my," she shyly said. "Are those for me?"

"Is there anyone else in the room?" He laughed as he followed her to the kitchen.

"But you just gave me flowers." She gestured towards the ones sitting on the plant stand.

"I saw these and knew they were meant for you."

She searched a cabinet for a vase, and just like before, she took his breath away. He was surprised that she'd left her hair loose tonight. Normally she wore it up in a high ponytail or a messy bun. He couldn't wait to run his fingers through it.

"Alejandro, these are gorgeous." She took a sniff. "And they smell so good. Thank you." He winked at her and her face lit up. He certainly hoped he wasn't misreading her actions. He believed she was as much into him as he was her.

"So what's for dinner?" He leaned against the counter and listened to her as she described in detail she'd prepared chicken breasts with a lemon marinade, angel hair pasta, and broccoli. He felt her excitement. "I take it you enjoy cooking."

She handed him the wine opener and reached for the glasses. "I do, although it's kind of hard cooking for one, so I generally make something that'll last a few days." He popped the cork and poured their glasses. "I haven't had someone to dinner for ages. I'm glad you were okay with not going out." She reached for her glass of wine, taking a sip. "It's more comfortable staying in than going to a crowded restaurant. We can talk freely without worrying about who may hear or see us." He noticed her fingering the edge of her wine glass.

"Is something wrong with the wine?"

"Oh no, it's fabulous."

"Then what's troubling you?" She pulled in her lips. He could tell she was wrestling with her words. A strand of her hair brushed against her mouth. He raised his hand and swept it aside, securing it behind her ear. He bent his knees so he could look her squarely in the eyes. "Tammy?" She began to gnaw on her lower lip. He placed his index finger there, attempting to stop her nervousness. He waited for her to answer his question, and when she didn't, he spoke instead. A broad smile broke out across his face. "Are you feeling what I'm feeling?" She continued to chew on her lip. "Tammy, I think what we have here is pretty special, and I hope you feel the same way."

He felt her hand as it grasped his. "Yes," she breathed. "Yes, I have feelings for you. I've never felt this way before." She glanced away from him then added, "Although, I think it's too soon. We hardly know one another. Our first date was just Saturday."

"True, but from what I've been told, when you meet the right woman, oftentimes one knows right away. I've never felt this way before, either. When we're apart, I can't wait to see you, and then when I'm with you, I'm counting the minutes until we can be together again. This makes absolutely no sense to me. I just know what I feel. You're becoming very import-ant to me."

"I feel the exact same way. It's like you've come out of nowhere and have swept me off my feet. Maybe we need to slow it down a little."

He rested his forehead against hers. "What are we going to do?"

"What I do know is, I don't want this to end. Ale-jandro, do you believe in love at first sight?"

"Are you telling me you've felt this way since our first meeting?"

She slapped at his arm. "No silly, but I have since our first date. I was seeing you with a different set of eyes—outside the hospital."

He cupped the side of her face. "I've never said this to anyone before, Tammy, but I think I'm falling in love with you." Her eyes began to fill. She did her best, but a tear escaped and slipped down her face. "Hey, what's this about? This is a happy time, not sad."

"I am happy. I never thought I'd hear those words coming from you, Alejandro. I'm just a plain old kind of girl. I never expected someone like you to fall in love with me."

"Why not?"

"First of all, you're a doctor— a successful one too. You're making such advances in medical science. I would have thought you'd have a million girls on your arm."

"Not a million, just you." He kissed the tip of her nose. "In fact, I've hardly dated since high school. Becoming a doctor has been my sole focus for as long as I can remember. In the last few days, I'm seeing life a little differently. I now know what it feels like to have that all-important someone in your life. Right now, I can't see the future without you in it." On that note, the timer dinged, signifying the chicken was done.

He couldn't take his eyes off her. The timer kept ringing in the background until she finally stepped away and turned it off. Grabbing a pair of oven mitts, she opened the oven. He'd reached for his wine when he heard her cry out. "Ouch, that hurt."

Setting his glass down, he hurried to her side. She'd dropped the oven mitts and was holding her hand. "Let me get that." He grabbed the mitts and pulled the chicken from the oven, then reached for her hand. "Let me take a look."

"Oh, it's nothing. I wasn't paying attention and put my fingertips on the oven rack. It's not my first burn nor will it be my last." He examined her hand just the same.

"Do you have some aloe you could put on it? It doesn't look too bad."

"See, what did I tell you?"

He knew she was in some pain and wanted to assist her. "Why don't you sit down, and I can put everything on the table."

"I'm fine, Alejandro. Sit. You're my guest." She went about getting the rest of their dinner onto the table while he watched. He wanted to help but felt he'd just be in the way. He'd offer to do the dishes; that way she'd keep her burn dry.

By the time she'd finished serving dinner, Alejandro had finished off his glass of wine. He retrieved the bottle from the counter, refilled his glass, and topped hers off. He rested his chin on his open palm as she sat down.

"What are you looking at?" she laughed.

"Nothing."

"You're staring at me. Do I have something on my face?" She ran her hand across it, then looked down at her sweatshirt. He knew she couldn't see a thing because what he saw was her inner beauty. "Alejandro, what is it?"

"You."

"Me? What about me?"

"You're so beautiful." A blush broke out across her face. He ran his fingertip across her cheek. "You're blushing."

"I am not."

"I think you are, and I love it."

She grabbed his hand and kissed it. "No one has ever said that to me."

"What? Told you that you're beautiful?" She lowered her eyes. "Hey, look at me. You are beautiful both inside and out. You are caring, compassionate, sweet, fun-loving— shall I go on?"

He tipped her head up so she could look at him. "Tammy, you're everything to me, if you haven't figured it out by now." He leaned over and kissed her soundly. His stomach grumbled. "I'm starving."

"I got the message. I'm hungry, too. Enjoy."

After they finished their meal, Alejandro grabbed the dishes. His arms were elbow deep in dish suds when his cell phone rang. He'd set it on the counter when he'd walked in. "Can you see whose calling?"

She reached for his cell and noticed it was the hospital. "It's the hospital."

"Answer it for me—put it on speaker."

"Dr. Alvarez." A female on the other end spoke. A concerned expression crossed Tammy's face when she heard they were calling about Frederick.

"His temperature's spiked, he's been spitting up…" They listened to Frederick's symptoms. Alejandro always monitored for signs of rejection.

"I'll be right there." He'd located a towel on the counter and was wiping his arms free of the dish suds.

"I'm going with you."

"You don't have to."

"I want to. I can be there for his parents."

He reached for her hands. "See why I said what I did earlier? You're always thinking about everyone else. You're always there for the family members, and I thank you for that."

"It's my job."

"You go above and beyond, Tammy. See what you're

doing tonight? You're off. It's not expected of you, yet you want to be there for them. That means a lot to me." Winking at her, he said, "Come on, let's go."

Chapter Three

IN MINUTES THEY WERE RUSHING down the hospital hallway towards the PICU. Alejandro immediately went into doctor mode, reviewing all of Frederick's information. He examined the baby boy and ordered a series of tests, but his gut told him it was an infection, rather than a rejection of the new heart.

Hours passed as Alejandro waited for the test results. Tammy sat huddled with Frederick's parents in the waiting room while they waited and waited for word on their son. It was just after one in the morning when Alejandro delivered the news he had hoped for. "I believe it's an infection. His temperature's returned to normal." Frederick's mother collapsed into her husband's arms. "He's stable. Why don't the two of you get some rest? You need to stay strong for him."

Frederick's parents thanked him and headed off to the room they were using at the hospital. "How about I call a cab for you," Alejandro said to Tammy as she wiped her hand across her brow. He knew she was exhausted.

"What about you?"

"I'm going to crash here tonight."

"I'll stay too."

"You don't have to."

"I want to."

"Follow me." He motioned her towards the elevators. In a matter of minutes they were walking into his office. He reached into this closet and pulled out a blanket and pillow. "Here," he led her to the couch. "Lie down and try to get some rest."

"Where are you going to sleep?"

"I'm going to check on a few things. I'll be right here at my desk." As she lay down, he covered her with the throw and kissed her brow.

"Wake me if anything changes." Almost as soon as she lay down, her eyes closed, and she drifted off. Alejandro stood watching her, wondering what it would feel like to lie next to her and wrap her in his arms. He knew he couldn't go there right now. He needed to remain focused on Frederick.

He sat at his desk and reached for a bottle of water. He took a drink and then tried concentrating on the file in front of him. After a while, his eyes glazed over and he dozed. He hadn't been asleep for long when he felt a hand brush against his shoulder. He was startled at first, not sure where he was, and then realized he was in his office and was leaning precariously to the right.

"Sorry to wake you, but I thought you were going to fall out of your chair."

"Thanks! Did you get some sleep?"

"I did. It's almost six. Would you care for coffee? I know I can certainly use one."

"That sounds good right about now." He stood, raising his arms above his head as he stretched out the kinks that had overtaken his back and shoulders. "That feels good," he grunted. "Shall we go to the cafeteria and get breakfast, too? Then I'll take you home."

"Shouldn't we check on Frederick?"

"Of course, we will right before we leave. One of my associates is on call for me, and he'll be taking over." He slid on the shoes he'd kicked off earlier and led her towards the door. "Thanks for helping with Frederick's parents."

"I wouldn't want to be anywhere but here, knowing his condition. I love that little boy, and I want to see him survive." He nodded at her comments as they walked out the door.

When they reached the cafeteria, Alejandro grabbed a tray and headed towards the food service line. "Let's put it all on here." He was starved and ordered an egg casserole, toast, and a fruit plate for himself while Tammy selected yogurt and fruit. As she poured their coffee, he watched her closely. She looked exhausted. "As soon as we're done here, I'm taking you home to bed." He noticed the surprised look on her face. Realizing how he phrased his comment, he winked at her and raised his hand to her face. "That didn't come out right."

"I knew what you meant. It's been a long day, and I know you got less sleep than I did. Let's eat and check on Frederick. Then we can leave."

As they approached the check-out, Tammy stood beside him holding their coffees.

"One tray?" Crystal asked Alejandro.

"Yep, and two coffees too," he added, pointing to Tammy holding their coffees. With a smile on her face, Crystal gave him the total. He paid and as they walked away, Alejandro softly said to Tammy, "Come to think of it, I wonder why she keeps smiling at me. I'd never seen her smile before the other day."

"I guess lately she's just been in a good mood." He led her back to the same table they previously used. As he turned to sit down, he glanced back at Crystal, realizing he'd never paid for a woman's meal before in the cafeteria— and now two days this week he'd done that. He imagined she smiled because of his gesture.

"What are your plans for this weekend?" Tammy asked as she ate a spoonful of yogurt.

"First of all, I'm going to get some sleep and then I have to clean."

"Clean? Can't that wait until you're rested more?"

"Unfortunately it can't. I don't think I told you, but my sister, Gabriella, is coming up next week for a few days."

"No, you didn't. Is there a particular reason why? Like is it your birthday?"

"Nothing like that." He took a bite of his toast. "She's a teacher and has a few days off. We haven't seen each other for some time, and she misses her big brother." He chuckled at his own comment. "I haven't seen her too much since I left for medical school. She's the only girl in the family, and I guess she just misses me."

"Do you have any other siblings?"

"I have two brothers, Alec and Joe, who are both pediatricians. They work for my father."

"Really? That's interesting. Why didn't you follow in your father's footsteps?"

"That was the plan until my best friend died in high school of renal failure. That's when I decided I was going to be a nephrologist. One thing led to another, and now my focus is being a transplant surgeon. I want to make a difference, and I think I am."

"You most certainly are. Look what you've done for Frederick and all of your other patients."

"Yeah, you're right."

"Was your father disappointed that you didn't become a pediatrician?"

"I don't think he was. He knew how close Jacob and I were. He understands why I chose what I did. He's just thankful that I followed him into medicine." He ran his hand along his face. He thought for a moment. "Are you working next Wednesday?"

"I'm not. I switched with one of the other nurses who needed Saturday off. Why?"

"Would you like to meet my sister? I've got to warn you, she can be a handful, but she'd do anything for you. She can be meddlesome, but she means well."

"I'd love to meet her."

He stacked their plates. "Let's go check on Frederick. Housework awaits me, you know."

"After a nap, right?"

He dropped off their plates at the dishwasher. As they strolled down the hallway towards the elevators, he laid his hand along her back. He realized it was the first time he'd gone through a crisis with one of his patients with someone by his side. He liked being able to share his concerns with someone that understood the situation— someone besides one of his peers.

They quickly checked on Frederick. Thankfully, he appeared to be resting comfortably and was stable. By eight, Alejandro had already dropped Tammy off and was sleeping soundly in his own bed. He'd set his alarm for noon but woke at ten. He decided not to waste time going back to sleep, so he took a quick shower and started in on his laundry and housecleaning.

He was looking forward to seeing Gabriella and knew he needed to make a conscious effort to return to St. Louis more often. In fact, maybe he'd head home for the holidays.

⁓

The next several days passed in a blur. He'd seen little of Tammy since he'd dropped her off after dealing with Frederick's latest crisis. Thankfully, the baby had stabilized and been moved out of the PICU unit. He and Tammy had passed each other in the hallway, but other than that, they'd only spoken on the phone. He looked forward to seeing her the following day.

Before he knew it Tuesday, Gabriella rang his door-bell. "Gabriella," he cheerfully said as he opened his door. "Come here and let me give you a hug."

She threw herself into his arms. "Alejandro, it's so good to see you. I've missed you." She kissed his cheek and walked into his home. "Before I forget, Mom and Dad said hello."

"Yeah, I know what that means."

"She didn't tell me to have you call her."

"No?" *Just informing me of her hello is enough in and of itself.* "In Momspeak, that means call her."

She laughed at his comment and threw her long hair over her shoulder. "Yeah, it does."

"Did you have a good trip?"

"I did. It's really not a bad drive. I'm glad to get out of town for a few days. It was a long summer, and I was busy as usual making games and such for my classroom."

"You work too hard. You earn every bit of your time off during the summer."

"I don't work as hard as you, Dad, Alec, or Joe."

"How can you say that when you're educating our leaders of tomorrow?"

"Well, I don't know about our next leaders, but I guess you're right. I do work hard during the school year. Enough about me working too hard, what's new with you?"

"Not much. I've been going pretty much non-stop myself this last month. I have some time off, if that's what you want to call it, over the next few weeks. I'm not on call."

"That's good. You need to slow down, enjoy life, and find a woman to spend some time with." He grinned at her comment. "Alejandro, is there something you've been keeping from me?"

He headed towards the kitchen. "What would you like to drink?"

"Alejandro, get back here. Are you dating someone?"

"What if I am?"

"Do I get to meet her?"

He spun around and went to the refrigerator and grabbed two bottles of water. Turning towards her, he handed her one. He liked to tease her and was doing just that right now.

"Alejandro, what's her name? Where did you meet? How long have you known her?"

"Enough with the questions, Gabriella."

"Well, I'm curious. Can't I be curious? I want to know all about her."

"Who said it's a 'her'?" He watched her eyes grow as large as saucers. He let her ponder his question for a few moments. He liked to taunt her but realized he didn't want to carry on his little joke too long. "I'm only kidding. Her name is Tammy, and I've known her for quite some time. We just started seeing one another, officially."

"Whew, I was worried there for a minute."

"Gabriella."

"Well, I was."

They sat down at the kitchen table and discussed everything and anything. He glanced at his watch. It was nearing seven, and he was getting hungry. "I'm starving. Let's go get something to eat."

"I'm hungry, too. Let's call Tammy and have dinner with her." Alejandro shook his head. She loved to get under his skin, and she was doing a pretty good job of it right now.

"Not tonight."

"I want to meet her. I'm only here for a couple of days."

"I realize that." He was going to string her along. He'd already made plans with Tammy for the following day. They were going to drive up north and look at the trees since the leaves had already started changing colors.

"Alejandro, are you ashamed of me that I can't meet your girlfriend?"

"Where did that come from? Why would you think I'm ashamed of you?"

"Well?"

"Well, what?" He realized she was sulking now. When she didn't immediately get her way, she often acted in this manner. "Just take a breath, Gabriella. Geesh! You're not even here twenty minutes and I'm about ready to send you back home." He was kidding with her, but all the same, she needed to know just because she was the youngest, she didn't always get her own way.

"Sorry. I'm just so excited to meet her. This is the first woman I've ever heard you mention that you were dating."

He walked over and pulled her into his arms. "All's forgiven." He released her and moseyed into his family room. "Anyway, she can't have dinner with us because she's working late tonight. You'll meet her tomorrow when we go out."

"I will? Oh you...You were just egging me on weren't you? You like to see me get all worked up."

"I do, and I miss it too. Grab your purse, and let's get something to eat. I'm sure you're tired after your drive." They headed out to a local diner. He knew she loved diner food as she often ate at the seventies-inspired diner that was just around the corner from their parents' home. By the time they finished their meal, it was close to nine. He drove her around the Capitol that was fully lighted. "I think the building is prettier at night than during the day."

"It is beautiful," she said as she clicked away on her camera. They drove around downtown a little longer, then, he headed home.

By the time they returned to his house, it was close to eleven. "I'm going to bed," she said yawning.

"See you tomorrow."

"Yep! Can't wait to meet Tammy."

"I'm sure you can't." He kissed her forehead and watched as she headed off to bed. He hoped she behaved herself the following day. She could be a handful and all he really wanted to do was focus on Tammy.

Chapter Four

GABRIELLA WAS UP AT THE crack of dawn. She was beside herself with excitement. She couldn't wait to meet Alejandro's girlfriend. She showered and dressed and was making her second cup of coffee when Alejandro greeted her with sleep-tousled hair and red-rimmed eyes.

"Look what the cat dragged in." She chuckled as he made his way to the coffee pot. "It looks like you went on a drunken binge and were up all night. What's up with that?"

He growled at her. "For your information, I didn't go on a drunken binge, and I look like this every morning when I wake up."

"I guess it's been awhile since I've seen you in this state, then." She snickered. "So when are we meeting Tammy? I've been up since five waiting on you."

"Gabriella, not this early," he glanced at the clock. "It's only…"

"Seven," she exclaimed. She leaned against the counter as she watched him make his coffee. "I forgot you liked creamer in your coffee. Is that something new?" He glared at her.

"Gabriella, it hasn't been that long since you've been in my presence. You're acting like you haven't seen me in years rather than weeks."

"Weeks? It's been three months since you last visited us, and that's only because Mom guilted you into it. Before that it was like six months since any of us had seen you."

"Okay, Gabby, I get your point. I've been busy. Busier than I've ever been. The transplant program at the hospital has taken off like gangbusters this year. I'm not going to apologize for my job."

"I don't expect you to. I just want you to be happy and to take care of yourself. From the looks of you, I'm not sure you're doing either one." She paused. "I guess I'll have an answer to one of my concerns when I get to lay my eyes on Tammy. So when are we meeting her?"

"Uhh, Gabriella." He looked again at the clock and shrugged. Then he picked up his phone, pulled up a number, and hit send.

She anxiously waited to see who he was calling. "Hey, it's me." She guessed he'd phoned Tammy. She was giddy with excitement and couldn't stand still. Jumping up and down like a teenager, she listened to him. "Can you be ready in like a half-hour?" He rubbed his hand across his forehead. "Yeah, I know I originally said I'd pick you up at ten but plans have changed. My sister is driving me crazy. She can't wait to meet you. I'll do anything to get her to settle down. How about breakfast?"

"Breakfast?" Gabriella practically yelled.

"Yep, that was my sister." He turned to her. "She heard you yelling in the background."

"I can't wait to meet you, Tammy," she called out.

He listened momentarily. "She heard that too, and she can't wait to meet you, either…" She listened further. "I'll be by at eight."

"That's more than a half-hour." Exasperated, she noticed him shake his head at her. "Well?"

"Gabriella, will you shush. I can barely hear Tammy."

"Okay, I'll be quiet."

"Yep, she's certainly excited to meet you. See you in a few." With coffee cup in hand, he hung up the phone and walked from the room.

"Alejandro?"

"Get dressed. We're leaving in a half hour."

"I am dressed."

"Good for you." She heard him slam his bedroom door.

"Well, he certainly got up on the wrong side of the bed," she exclaimed to herself as she took a sip of her coffee.

Fifteen minutes later, Alejandro reappeared and found Gabriella sitting quietly in the family room. "Now, what's wrong?"

"Nothing, why do you ask?"

"You're being awfully quiet."

"Didn't you tell me to shush earlier?"

"I did. Gabriella, I miss you when you're not here, but right now, I could send you a packin'."

She jumped from the couch and flung her arms around him. "I love you, too, big brother. Now, shall we?"

"Shall we what?"

"Go get your girl."

He shook his finger at her. "You'd better behave. This is the last time I'm going to warn you. This is my house and I can kick you out."

"You wouldn't dare."

"I wouldn't?" He smiled broadly and reached for his car keys. "Let's go."

"I think someone woke up on the wrong side of the bed."

"Who me?"

She waggled her finger at him as she walked out the door. "Yes, you. I certainly hope Tammy is more amenable to your attitude than I am." She threw her hair over her shoulder, slapping him in the face with it.

She knew she was getting under his skin but loved every minute of it. She missed him more than words could say, and she hoped someday he'd move back home. She needed his guidance in her life. When she was a little girl and she'd misbehaved or did something stupid, he always knew how to make her feel better. She missed their talks and being around him more and more as she got older. *Maybe someday he'll come home.*

~

Promptly at eight o'clock he pulled into Tammy's driveway. He opened his car door and turned to his sister who sat in the backseat. Shaking his finger at her again, he said, "You stay here, and you need to behave, Gabriella. I mean it. I'll send you home."

Saluting him, "Yes, sir," she sternly said as he closed the door, then she broke into a fit of laughter as he walked away from the car. Turning back, he pursed his lips and shook his head at her and then proceeded to the door. He knew she was taunting him and enjoying every minute of it. He needed to relax and not let her get the best of him. He'd waited days to be in Tammy's presence outside of the hospital, and he wanted to enjoy every minute of it.

He rang the doorbell and waited. It took Tammy longer than he expected to answer. She held her shoes in her hand and looked like she'd been fooling with her hair. "Come on in. I still need to finish getting ready."

He walked through the door and pulled her into his arms. Kissing her soundly on the lips, he said, "Be prepared for my sister. She is definitely in rare form."

"She sounds like fun."

"Glad you think so."

"Alejandro, give it a rest. She's just playing around with you."

"If you say so...Don't forget that I warned you in advance."

"I won't. In fact, I can't wait to meet her. I think we'll hit it right off." He hung his head as he waited for her to finish putting her shoes on.

"Grab a coat too. It's a little chilly today."

"Thanks." She leaned in, brushing her lips to his. "I missed you too." She tapped her hand on his cheek and started out the door.

"Sweetheart, I missed you, I did. I apologize. Gabriella's just got me all riled up."

"I understand, dear. Now, take me to your unruly sister."

By the time he'd escorted Tammy down the sidewalk, Gabriella had exited the car and was waiting with open arms. "Hi, Tammy, I'm Gabriella."

"Gabby, didn't I tell you to stay in the car?"

"Oh shush, you. I'm being welcoming." She pulled Tammy into a hug. "I'm glad we could finally meet."

Alejandro watched his sister hug the woman he loved.

In fact, he was watching two of the most important women, outside of his mother, that he could honestly say he loved. "Okay Gabby, I think the welcoming party is about over. We need to get going if we're going to have breakfast."

"Okay, let's eat," she cheerfully said as she got back in the car. He waited for Tammy to get situated and then closed the door. He couldn't believe the antics of his sister. *She's definitely going to keep me on my toes today*, he thought as he opened his car door.

They enjoyed breakfast, and he was surprised that Gabriella actually behaved herself. She asked Tammy about her family and her job. He wasn't a bit surprised with how warm Tammy was with Gabriella. She didn't get flustered by all of his sister's questions, and she'd definitely asked quite a few. She'd held her own against Gabriella, and he was proud of her as his sister was definitely a handful on good days.

He chuckled to himself when Tammy did an about face on Gabriella and started throwing questions back at her. They were definitely a match made for one another, and he enjoyed watching them go back and forth.

"Hey, where'd you go?" He felt Tammy's hand on his arm before he heard her words.

"I'm right here."

"No, silly. You had this blank look on your face."

"Well, of course I did, listening to you two banter back and forth."

"Alejandro?" Gabriella said.

"Well?" he said.

"At least we're getting along and talking. You haven't said one word since we sat down."

"I have too."

"What? I'll have an omelet." He had to laugh at Gabriella's statement. "It's true."

Waving his hand about, he said, "I didn't want to interrupt your scintillating conversation." Gabriella and Tammy both had to laugh. "Are you finished? I'd like to get on the road sometime today." They'd been sitting in the restaurant for almost two hours chatting away, at least Tammy and Gabriella had been.

"I'm ready, what about you, Gabby?" Tammy stood.

"Yep, just let me take one last swallow of my coffee."

"I think you've had a gallon of coffee today," Alejandro said. "You'd better not make me stop every five minutes for you to go to the bathroom."

"I won't," she exclaimed, crossing her fingers behind her so he couldn't see. He knew what she was like—always needing to stop for a bathroom break. Hopefully today would be different.

Two hours later, Alejandro sat shaking his head. "I can't believe it. This is the third time we've stopped for her."

"Alejandro, lighten up. It's not a big deal." Tammy smiled when he leaned over and caressed her cheek. "I'm enjoying her. She's a breath of fresh air. Nothing seems to bother her."

"Yah think? Plenty bothers her. She's in a really good mood today, and I'm glad to see it. She's had a rough time the last few years, and it's nice to see her happy."

"Here she comes."

Gabriella opened her door. "Thanks for stopping, Alejandro. I'm sorry I drank so much coffee this morning. I didn't think."

"It's not a problem, Gabby. Now, are you ready to enjoy the trees?"

They wound their way along the Wisconsin River, enjoying the rapidly changing leaves. "This is beautiful. Do you get up here often?" Gabriella inquired as he drove along a two lane highway.

"I love to come up here to fish. A friend of mine has a boat, and we take it out every so often. What I like about this area is that it's peaceful and not too crowded. During the summer months, it's pretty hectic up here."

He drove along and came across one of the many pumpkin farms in the area. "It seems like the pumpkin farms all have corn mazes now, doesn't it?" Gabriella said.

"Up here it's quite common, that's for sure."

"Do you remember going apple picking at Lapinsky's Orchard when we were kids?" she asked.

"I do. I also remember the pumpkin patch. What was the name of it?"

"Olson's. The kindergartners from school just went there this week. I hear they have a corn maze now, too. According to one of the teachers, it's huge, and they have so many activities for the kids. When we went, it was just a big old pumpkin patch."

Alejandro realized Tammy had been quiet for the last several miles. "Tammy, did you ever go to the pumpkin patch?"

"Yeah, we did when I was in school, and I also went with the Girl Scout troop I was in."

"Did you sell cookies too?"

"I did and I even was the highest cookie seller in our entire troop of twenty girls."

"You must have sold a lot."

"I did. I think I sold close to a thousand boxes."

"Wow, I can't imagine delivering all of them."

"I didn't have to. My dad did."

Gabriella laughed at her comment.

"Sounds like Dad, doesn't it Gabby."

"Yep, my dad sold my cookies all over the hospital, and he almost killed me when he had to deliver them all…Gosh, I haven't thought about that in a long time."

He slowed the car as they approached a little town. "Who's hungry?"

"I could get something to drink," Tammy said as he neared a local restaurant.

"Let's make this a pit stop, Gabby," he claimed, looking in the rear view mirror.

"I don't have to go."

"Well, you'd better try before we leave." He felt a tap on his head as Gabriella leaned over the seat and bonked him.

"I haven't had to go in almost an hour."

"Let's keep it that way."

They enjoyed a late lunch at the Goose Point Inn. It was a small establishment off the beaten path. By the time they finished, it was nearing four. "It's getting late, and the sun's going to set shortly."

"Thanks, Alejandro. This was a lovely ride," Gabriella commented as he turned around and headed back to town.

"Would you like to come over for a bit?" he asked Tammy.

"I'd love to, but I've got laundry to finish. After all, we started out a couple of hours earlier than we planned."

"Sorry about that, Tammy. I was just so excited to meet you that I didn't let up until Alejandro called you. It's my fault."

"Don't worry about it, Gabby. I'm glad we got to meet and have this outing together." She reached into her purse and pulled out a slip of paper and a pen. "Here, write your information down. I'd love to stay in touch with you."

"Same here," Gabby said as they exchanged their contact information.

By the time they finished swapping their addresses and phone numbers, Alejandro was pulling up to Tammy's house. "I'll see you in," he said as he looked back at Gabriella. He needed a few moments with Tammy.

"I'm so glad we got to meet." Gabriella gave Tammy a goodbye hug. "Please stay in touch. Maybe my brother here will bring you to St. Louis soon."

Alejandro had approached her side and reached for her hand. "I hope to see you soon too." He smiled at Tammy as she grabbed onto his hand.

He opened her door for her and saw her inside. "Sorry about that."

"What's there to be sorry about? I absolutely love her. She's fun!"

"I'm glad you think so." He pulled her into his arms. "I've wanted to hold you like this all day, but I couldn't."

"Gabby wouldn't have cared."

"Oh no! She would have run right home with the news that we were getting married."

"Alejandro, she's not that bad. I find her refreshing." He kissed her upturned lips and growled. "I wish we had a little more alone time today. The rest of the week is going to be a bear. I know I won't have time to take you out."

"I understand." She hugged him close. "This is nice, but now I need to let you go so your inquiring-minds sister won't wonder what we were doing in here for so long."

He pulled away slightly and kissed the tip of her nose. "I'll try and phone you tomorrow, but..."

"We'll talk when we talk, okay?"

He nodded his head as he turned to walk out the door. He needed one more kiss so he lunged towards her and pulled her hard against his chest. "I'm going to miss you."

"I'm not going anywhere. I'll be here when you have time."

He stroked the side of her face and kissed her one last time before heading out the door.

He'd had a fun day. Gabriella had settled down and had gotten along famously with Tammy. He felt good about their day as he got back into the car.

"She loves you."

"Huh?"

"I said she loves you and you love her."

"Where did that come from?"

"I know what I saw, and you two are hopelessly in love."

"Now, don't go share that with Mom. All I need for her to do is call wondering when the wedding is and why I haven't introduced her to Tammy yet."

"Don't worry, I won't say a thing. Like I said, I want to see you happy, and I believe I have my answer." She leaned over and kissed his cheek. "I think you're good together, and I hope it all works out because you deserve it." Alejandro smiled at her. She liked seeing him smile again. He seemed relaxed and happy something she'd hadn't seen in him in a long time.

"What's on the agenda tomorrow?" she asked as he drove home.

"Work, for me."

"I'll make dinner. What time do you think you'll be

home?"

"Hard to say."

"I'll figure something out. We have to eat."

"I'm sure you will."

He wasn't surprised the next morning when he was again greeted by a cheerful Gabriella.

"What time do you eat lunch?" she asked.

"I don't know. I have a surgery first thing, why?"

"I thought I'd come by."

"You don't have to. I'll just see you tonight." With that, he grabbed a cup of coffee and headed out the door. He knew by the look on her face that she was up to no good. He could only imagine what her plans for the day were.

Alejandro had barely walked out the door when she phoned Tammy. "So what time's lunch?"

"Oh hi, Gabby. I eat around one, why?"

"I'd like to join you, if that's alright with you."

"Sure, that sounds like fun. How about I meet you in the cafeteria? That'll be easier."

"Sure thing. See you at one."

Gabriella met Tammy promptly at one outside the cafeteria. "Thanks for agreeing to meet me."

"I'm glad you called. I normally eat by myself, so this is a treat for me."

"You don't eat with my brother?"

"We have on occasion, but we're trying to keep our relationship on the down-low here at the hospital."

"Gotcha." They went through the cafeteria line and were lucky enough to find a table towards the back of the room. "I couldn't leave without saying a proper goodbye, Tammy. I had a blast yesterday, and I hope I wasn't too much trouble."

"Gabby, why would you say that? I'm so happy I got to meet you. I had a really nice time."

"I'm glad. I know Alejandro wasn't too happy with me. I hate it when I disappoint him."

"Why would you say that?"

"Just because. Anyway, I'm going to tell you what I told my brother last night, and I hope I'm not over-stepping myself." She reached for Tammy's hand. "I like you a lot Tammy, and I think you're the best thing that's happened to my brother in a long time." Smiling at her, Gabby couldn't hold back her true impression. "I think you love my brother, and I'm almost posi-tive he loves you. Am I close here?" She watched a blush creep up Tammy's face. "I won't pressure you, but what I do want to say is, I hope this works out with you two. I know I can be a little overzealous at times, and I apologize if I was that way at all yesterday. My brother means the world to me. I miss him so much. But what I want you to know is, I'm happy for the two of you, and if things work out, I'd love to have you for my sister."

"Gabby, we haven't dated very long."

"It doesn't matter to me how long you've dated him. I know love when I see it, and you two are head over heels in love with one another. I just wanted you to know I'd be thrilled for you to be a member of our family." She took a drink of her iced tea. "One last thing…I promised my brother, and I'm making the same promise to you. I won't say a word about your relationship to my family. It's up to the two of you to make or break it, and I don't want my mother leaning on Alejandro, encouraging him one way or another.

I'm in your corner, and I hope you take it to the next level. As I said, I'd love to call you my sister."

Tammy's lunch hour flew by and before Gabriella knew it, she was saying goodbye. She pulled Tammy into a tight hug. "I hope to see you soon." She smiled at Tammy and watched her walk down that hallway. She knew the pretty nurse was good for Alejandro and hoped that one day she'd be able to call her sister.

Chapter Five

TIME FLEW BY AND BEFORE they knew it, the holidays were practically upon them. Tammy and Alejandro had spent almost every waking hour together outside of the hospital. After Gabriella's visit, they decided to go to the Columbia County pumpkin patch, where one of the largest corn mazes in the state was cut. It stayed open well past Halloween, closing right before Thanksgiving. They warmed by the bonfire before taking their foray into the maze and had a fantastic time even when they got lost in the middle of it.

After leaving the pumpkin patch, they headed through the windy, hilly countryside that ran along the Wisconsin River. Tammy thought they were returning home via a different route. She really wasn't paying attention as he drove along— that is until he turned down the highway where Prairie Wines was located.

It was one of the larger wineries in the area and overlooked the Wisconsin River. The other day when they'd been discussing places to visit in the area, she'd mentioned to Alejandro that she wanted to tour one of the local wineries. As they drove through the expansive gates, she noticed the grape vines that were planted along the hillside as far as the eye could see. She'd researched the winery and knew that it sat atop cool limestone caverns that allowed the company to age wines in oak barrels. She sat in awe as he drove along towards the stone building that housed the tasting room.

"I can't believe you brought me here."

"You said you wanted to tour the winery. I thought this would be the perfect way to end our day after the corn maze. I wanted it to be a surprise."

"It definitely is."

"I'm glad. You ready to taste some wine?"

"You mean we need fortification after getting lost in that maze?"

"That too." He parked the car and hurried her along. "Come on, Tammy." He grabbed ahold of her hand as he'd made reservations for them. "We're on the three o'clock tour."

"We are?" He pulled her alongside him as they entered the winery store. She was astonished and couldn't believe he'd arranged the tour for them.

They arrived just in time to join the group as they headed out. Their first stop was a video, showcasing the winery's history. Next, they walked outside past the vineyards and then toured the limestone aging cellars. After she'd seen the tempting barrels aging some of her favorite wines, she was more than ready to sample them.

By the time they'd completed their wine tasting, she was starved. After spending the majority of the day outside soaking up the late fall sunshine, all she wanted to do was enjoy a quiet dinner with Alejandro. She waited while he purchased a case of wine and loaded it into the trunk of the car. As he eased the trunk closed, she wrapped her arms around him from behind. Nuzzling his back, she squeezed him tightly. "Thank you for this. It was such a surprise."

"You said you wanted to visit the winery. I knew it was close enough to the pumpkin patch, so I decided to add it into my plans for day."

"By the sound of that, I have to believe you have..."

He turned in her arms, leaned in, and kissed her nose. "I do." He glanced at his watch. "We have reservations in twenty minutes."

"Reservations? Where?"

"If I told you, it wouldn't be a surprise now, would it?" Kissing her soundly on the lips, he swatted her behind. "Get in the car. I don't want to be late."

"Yes, sir," she exclaimed as she jumped into the car beside him. Leaning over, she cupped the side of his face, "This has been *the* perfect day, and I mean it. Thank you."

"It's not over yet."

He drove a short way and turned off the highway. *Another lovely surprise* she thought as he pulled into a well-known steak house. The building was an old stone home that was surrounded by tall mature trees. If one didn't know it was a restaurant, one would think it was an old home with history. Built in the eighteen hundreds, Stonewall was known throughout the area for its succulent steaks and Friday night fish fry. In past lives, Stonewall was a tavern, general store, and a stagecoach resting area. She knew if the walls could talk, the place would be filled with all kinds of stories.

They were immediately escorted to a table. She rested her chin on her upturned palm while she listened to him order a bottle of wine. As she replayed their day, a slow smile broke across her face. She'd believed their trip to the pumpkin patch had been spontaneous on his part, without thought, but boy was she wrong. He'd planned the entire day in extreme detail. As her smile intensified, she realized how lucky she was to have him in her life. She still couldn't believe she was dating Dr. Alejandro Alvarez. She knew by word of mouth that he was slated to become the next head of the department. At his young age, that was a monumental accomplishment. She shook her head, still in awe that he was hers.

"Is something wrong?"

"No, oh no."

"Then why the look?"

"I was just thinking about our day and how special it's been."

He reached across the table grabbing her hand. Raising it to his lips, he brushed a kiss across her knuckles. "I'm so glad you've enjoyed your day. You deserved it."

Before she could say another word, they were interrupted by the waiter who'd brought their bottle of wine. She watched as Alejandro sampled it. Life was good, and she was happy he was a part of it.

Both of their schedules dictated that they work the Thanksgiving holiday weekend. When the schedule was initially set, he wasn't dating Tammy, and he couldn't have cared less if he worked the holiday or not. Since he had no family in Madison, he would spend the day quietly at home. Now things were different, but instead of dwelling on it, he looked forward and was ever thankful that he'd planned a trip back home during Christmas week. He had arranged ten days off and would spend a good chunk of it with his family. He hadn't broached the subject with Tammy yet, but he hoped she'd be able to go with him.

Alejandro was finishing up the last of his notes when he heard a soft knock on his office door. It was late and all of his staff had gone home for the day. He hadn't seen Tammy in a couple of days since she'd been working nights. Three nights ago, he'd had a late surgery, and he'd been able to catch up with her for only a few minutes. Other than that, they hadn't spent more than fifteen minutes together for almost a week. He opened the door and was pleasantly surprised to see her bright but tired-looking face staring back at his.

He immediately reached for her hand, drawing her into his office and into a warm embrace. "Hey, there," he softly said as he kissed her forehead. Leaning back he ran his hand along her jaw, her nape, and then into her hair before he dropped a sweet kiss to her lips. He slid his fingertip underneath her eyes, outlining the dark circles. "You look tired."

"I'm exhausted. It's not like I haven't worked this shift before. I can't figure out what's up with that— why I'm so fatigued. I guess I'm just getting older."

He led her towards the couch where they sat down. He pulled her back into his arms and kissed her again.

"I thought you were off tonight," he said as he tucked her into his side. "You've worked seven nights straight."

"Yeah, don't remind me." She nestled her head into the crook of his shoulder. "Gosh, I've missed you, and this." She raised her hand grabbing ahold of his shirt and then snuggled closer into his warmth. "I have a quick question for you before I head off to the floor. Would you like to come over for Thanksgiving?"

"Ah, well, don't you need to get some rest? And when, may I ask, will you have time to cook?"

She closed her eyes and shook her head. "That didn't come out right. I'm so tired I'm really not sure what I said. I certainly hope I get through tonight without any problems...What I meant was, my parents have invited us for dinner. Would you like to spend some of your day with me and meet my family?"

"I'd love to. What time do you typically eat? It would have to be late in the afternoon for me."

"That's not a problem. We don't celebrate our big meal until dinnertime."

"I guess it's a date then."

She smiled up at him and cleared her throat. "Thank you. I can't wait to introduce you to my family."

"Well, since we're discussing the holidays, what does your December schedule look like?"

She sighed deeply. "For once I had the foresight to plan ahead. I requested the last two weeks of the year off, and surprisingly, I got it."

He ran his hand through her hair, down her arm, and along her hip and thigh. "I'd love it if you could spare some of your vacation and come home with me. I think it's time you meet my family too." He'd been thinking about their next steps for days now. She was constantly in his thoughts morning, noon, and night. He couldn't get her out of his mind and didn't want to.

He felt her tense slightly in his arms. "Hey, it's okay if you think it's too soon to meet my family."

"Oh no, where did you get that idea?" She rested her hand against her temple.

"It seemed like you were pondering my question a

little longer than I expected, that's all."

She smiled at him and reached for his hand. "It's not that at all. I'd love to meet them. Mentally, I was trying to recall if I'd set up any appointments while I was off. If I did, I'll just cancel."

She ran her hand along his cheek. "Alejandro, I'd be honored to meet your family. If your parents or brothers are anything like Gabriella…"

He raised his hand, quieting her thoughts. "I need to warn you in advance. They are the direct opposite of my sister. My dad, Joe, and Alec are more reserved and they definitely won't talk your arm off like Gabriella. My mother's a different story. I'd say she's a cross between them.

"Either way, I can't wait to meet your family because if they're anything like you, I'm sure I'll love them as much as I love you." Oops. He said the words that had been right on the cusp for so long now. Thankfully, she took them in stride and didn't realize the feelings that he'd declared.

She patted his chest, looked at the clock, and groaned. "I've gotta go, or I'll be late for my shift." She wrapped her arms around him, squeezing him. "This is my last night, and then I return to days, thank God. Maybe I'll be able to catch up on my sleep."

"I can't wait. I've missed spending my free time with you. I feel like we haven't had one moment together for weeks."

"It's only been seven days, Alejandro."

"I realize that, but it seems like a lifetime." She kissed him one last time and shakily stood. His expression changed to one of concern. "Hey," he said, looking her directly in the eyes. "Are you going to make it tonight? You seem a little wobbly there."

"I'll be just fine. Once I hit the floor, my adrenaline will kick in, and before I know it, morning will be here." She glanced away. "At least I hope that's how it goes." He kissed her one more time and led her to the door. "I'll talk to you tomorrow."

"Sure thing." He watched her amble down the hallway towards the elevators, moving significantly slower than her normal breakneck pace. He didn't quite believe her optimism. Seven days on without a day off was difficult in and of itself, but make it a late night shift and that made it even more difficult, especially when you were used to working days.

It took Alejandro longer than he expected to finish his notes. It was late for him, almost midnight. He had the following day off, so before leaving the hospital, he decided to run by the PICU and check on Tammy. Frederick had been released from the hospital weeks ago, so he had no reason to visit the unit other than to see her. It didn't matter. He needed to make sure she was all right. He'd been concerned with how tired she'd looked.

As he approached the nurses' station, he noticed her almost immediately. He stood off to the side observing her. She seemed sluggish as she moved about the desk. She brushed her hand across her brow and then reached for her throat as she once again cleared it. The shadows beneath her eyes had intensified, and she seemed paler than she'd been only a few short hours ago.

As he began to approach the desk, she reached for a bottle of water. As she drank, she seemed to have difficulties swallowing. He wondered if she had a sore throat.

He startled her when he pressed his hand to her back.

Losing her balance, she fell into him. "Oh, Alejandro, where did you come from?"

"I've been standing over there watching you for the last five minutes."

"You have? I didn't see you."

He again pressed his hand to her back and guided her to an empty conference room. Closing the door behind him, he said, "What's going on?"

He could see the confusion on her face. "What do you mean what's going on?" She brushed her brow again, but this time he noticed a fine sheen of moisture dotting her forehead. "I don't understand your question."

He raised his hand to her forehead already knowing what the outcome would be. "Tammy, you're sick. You have a fever."

She flung her hand in front of her face, "I'm fine. There's nothing wrong with me." She'd barely finished her statement when she started coughing. Fisting her hand against her throat, she did her best to clear it and swallow.

"Don't tell me you're not ill. In the few seconds I've been in your presence, I've noticed your fatigue and your coughing. I believe you have a sore throat, and you have a fever."

"I don't have a fever."

"Shall we take your temperature?" Wide-eyed she looked at him. "Get your things, I'm taking you home."

"Alejandro, I'm fine." He turned and started out the door. "Where are you going?"

"To get a thermometer." She shrugged her shoulders at him. "Coming?"

She followed him to the desk where her supervisor just happened to be working on a chart. "I'm not feeling well, Camilla, and I need to go home."

"Tammy, I was just about to ask you how you felt. You look awfully pale."

"Yeah, I know. Since my shift started, I've developed a sore throat and a cough."

"Could be the flu," Camilla stated as she glanced back and forth between her and Alejandro. "Go home, get some rest, and I'll cover for you."

"Thank you, Camilla. I really appreciate it."

Alejandro waited as she grabbed her coat and purse. "She has a fever, too, but she's too stubborn to take her temperature."

"I thought she might, but Tammy's a dedicated nurse. She mustn't be feeling well if she agreed to go home without a fight."

"She and I had a little tiff, but when I threatened taking her temperature, she caved in pretty quickly."

Alejandro took one look at her as she walked from the employee lounge and knew that she was sicker than he'd first thought. She made her way to his side where he immediately placed his arm around her. "Let's get you home."

She turned back to Camilla. "Thanks for covering for me."

"Not a problem. Go home and get well." Alejandro led her down the hallway towards the bank of elevators. She leaned on him as they waited for the chime signifying one had arrived.

Before she knew it, he'd driven her home and was walking her up the sidewalk. He grabbed her keys from her hand and opened the door. "I appreciate the ride home." He helped her into her house and closed the door behind them.

"Do you need help getting changed?" She looked at

him with a perplexed expression on her face. "Honey,
I'm not going anywhere. Go get changed while I run
out to my car for my go bag. I'll be right back." In her
state of confusion, she apparently didn't understand. "I
have a change of clothes in the car. I'm spending the
night."

"Oh, you are?"

"I'm not leaving your side."

He ran to his car and returned in under thirty seconds with his change of clothes and his medical bag.
She was standing in the exact same place. "Tammy?"

"Alejandro, you don't have to stay. I'll be fine."

"Just humor me, okay? You're sick and I'm not leaving your side."

While he changed in the guest room, she made her
way to her bedroom. Fifteen minutes later he found
her sitting on the edge of her bed still dressed. He
squatted down in front of her and reached for her forehead. It was hotter than when he first felt her at the
hospital. He withdrew a thermometer from his pocket
and handed it to her. "Here, let's see how high your
temperature is."

While he waited for the thermometer to beep, he
noticed a pair of sweats and a t-shirt lying across her
bed. He grabbed them and handed them to her. He
heard the beep and took the thermometer. "No fever,
huh? Try 102.2. Now get changed."

He left her to dress while he went to the kitchen to
get a glass of cold water. He returned with not only
that but a fever suppressant as well. "Take these and
hop into bed." For once she listened to him. "No
wonder you were so fatigued. You've got the flu."

"It's too early in the season for that."

"You think? Think again. We'll have you tested

tomorrow if you're not feeling better. Rest and plenty of fluids are what the doctor orders for you."

"Yes, sir," she said as she was overtaken by a coughing fit.

"I'm glad I came up to check on you before I headed home. Knowing you, you would have finished out your shift."

"To be honest, I don't think I would have made it." He pulled the covers around her. "I'll be right here if you need me."

"You really should go home. You don't need to get sick too." He could see the light fade from her eyes.

"I'm just where I need to be. Taking care of the woman I love." In a matter of seconds, she'd drifted off to sleep. She hadn't realized that he'd again used the word love as in 'I love you.'

Tammy had a sitting area in the corner of her room. He grabbed a blanket and curled up on the chaise lounge that was nestled into the corner. As he lay there, he listened to her even breathing. He was thankful that she'd fallen into what appeared to be a peaceful slumber. Sleep was what she needed.

Before he knew it, he was awakened by a fit of coughing. He looked at his watch and discovered that it was just after three. He jumped up from the chaise and hurried to her side. Brushing her hair from her face, he felt her, to discover that her fever hadn't gone away. She opened her eyes at him.

"Hi! You're still here."

"What did I tell you? I'm taking care of the woman I love." Again the words 'I love you' slipped from his mouth. He was certain that she hadn't comprehended what he'd said. He realized then and there that he needed to tell her how he felt, but now definitely wasn't the right time.

"Yeah, I heard what you said—" He noticed her difficulty as she swallowed. He grabbed the glass of water that was sitting on her end table and handed it to her. "Thanks." She took a sip and then another. "I needed that."

"You still have a fever, and you can't have another round of aspirin for another couple of hours."

"I know." She started hacking again. "This cough came out of nowhere." She cleared her throat. "And now I have a sore throat."

"I think you were working on that when you were in my office. You kept clearing your throat."

"I did? I wasn't aware."

He slid the covers back over her and leaned down, kissing her brow. "Go back to sleep and hopefully when you wake you'll be feeling all better."

"I can wish, right?" He sat down on the edge of the bed as she settled in. Brushing one last kiss against her forehead, he watched her drift off. He stroked her arm as she slept, letting her know that he was there taking care of her. As he watched her, he knew she was the one for him. He loved her with a passion that he hadn't known he had inside of him. She was his everything, and he'd do whatever it took to make her feel better. He was glad he was off the following day. He'd be able to nurse her back to health.

Chapter Six

ALEJANDRO SPENT THE FOLLOWING DAY by her side as she recovered from the flu. By the time she felt well again, the holiday had arrived. Thanksgiving Day was busy for both of them. They arranged to leave the hospital after her shift ended and head over to her parents' house for dinner.

He'd been lucky and only had a handful of patients in the hospital that day, so he waited for her in his office. He'd phoned his parents and spoke with his entire family. He broke the news to his mother that he would visit during Christmas and that he planned on bringing his girlfriend to meet them.

As Alejandro waited for Tammy's shift to end, he recalled the excitement in his mother's voice when she realized he was bringing Tammy with him. He'd heard Gabriella screaming in the background when his mother relayed his news to his father.

"Your sister is awfully excited."

"I could tell."

"Are you keeping something from me?"

"Not that I can think of... Other than Gabriella met

Tammy when she was here last month."

"She did?"

"Yeah, and I can see she kept our secret. That's surprising."

"Alejandro," she chastised him. "Your sister can keep a secret." They spoke for a few minutes longer.

"I'll phone you in a few days when things settle down here, and we'll make arrangements for the visit."

"That sounds wonderful, son. I look forward to it."

He hung up the phone with a smile on his face, and then he realized he'd been smiling a lot lately. He owed it all to Tammy.

It seemed like the remainder of the day flew by. They left for her parents' house right at three when her shift ended. As they drove further and further out into the rural countryside surrounding Madison, Alejandro grew a tad bit nervous. Since he hadn't dated seriously since high school, he hadn't had the need to meet any of his dates' parents. When he'd gone out in high school, most of his girlfriends he'd grown up with, so he didn't need to worry about meeting the dreaded parents.

He knew she was aware of his nervousness when she turned to him. "Something wrong?"

"No, why?"

"You look like you're ready to meet the firing squad." He groaned. "My parents aren't going to bite."

"I know. It's been quite some time since I've met the 'parents', and I have to say it is a little daunting."

"Really?"

"Yes, really." He looked out of the corner of his eyes at her. "Here I am meeting the parents of the woman I love and..." She gasped. "What's wrong?"

"You love me?" He realized that the words came

without him even thinking about them and that she'd actually heard them this time, unlike his earlier fly-by comments. He'd felt this way for so long, they were just apart of him. He'd wanted the first time he told her to be special and not thrown into a normal conversation, so he pulled to the side of the road.

Reaching for her hand, he drew it to his lips. "Yes, I love you. I've loved you for so long that the words just slipped out without me even thinking about them. I didn't want to tell you too soon because I wasn't sure how you felt."

"Oh, Alejandro, I love you too, and I have since our first date, maybe even before. I didn't want to say anything myself because our relationship was so new. Yeah, you told me you thought you were falling in love with me but never said another word, so I wasn't sure if you were or not. Anyway, who falls in love this quickly?"

"We do," he said, laughing at her words. He ran the tip of his finger along her jawline. Leaning in, he brushed his lips against hers. She moaned as their lips touched. "Something wrong?"

"Oh no, everything is perfect." She wrapped her hand around his nape and kissed him soundly. "This is the best day ever. It truly is a day of Thanksgiving." She ended their kiss. "We'd better hit the road or else we'll miss dinner." He latched onto her hand and held it the remainder of the way.

They pulled into her parents' driveway just after three thirty. He squeezed her hand one more time before exiting the car. It was now or never, he thought as he opened her door. He was taken aback by his nervousness. It had come out of nowhere as they'd driven along. In their short trip, he'd discovered how in tune to one another they'd become with her picking up on his tenseness. He guessed that was one aspect of love that he was learning.

She led him through the kitchen door into a cook's kitchen where they were greeted with the aromas of a roasted turkey. It smelled wonderful. He stood back as she reached for her mother. Hugging her, she then reached back for Alejandro's hand. She grabbed it tightly and pulled him close. "Mom, I'd like to introduce you to Alejandro Alvarez."

"Mrs. Johansen," he said.

"I'm not your mother, Alejandro. Please call me Phyllis."

"Phyllis it is then." He shook her hand. In a matter of seconds, he found himself flanked not only by her father, Mark, but her siblings as well. Immediately, he felt at home, a part of this family. The nerves that once had slightly taken over had dissipated. Gone with a handshake.

Before he knew it, he was driving Tammy home. "I had a really good time."

"So, I guess your nerves were for nothing, right?"

"I can't say that." She looked at him strangely. "During my time of duress, we did convey our love for one another, so I can't say my nervousness was for nothing."

"You're right there."

"I have to say your mom and dad are very welcoming. Your brother and sister are nothing like I imagined. Max is a hoot. He definitely enjoys his football."

"That he does."

"And Elsa is so quiet. She's definitely the antithesis of Gabriella."

She snickered. "You can certainly say that."

He reached for her hand as he drove along. "I spoke with my mom today. We're going to make plans later in the week for our visit."

"That sounds nice. I'm looking forward to our trip."

"Are you okay staying at my parents'? I could always just get us a hotel room."

He felt her eyes on him and glanced her way. They'd discussed taking their relationship to the next level, but she wanted to wait. "It would be two rooms," he assured her. "I listened to what you said, and I understand you want to wait for us to make love. I won't pressure you into anything you don't want to do. I promise."

She squeezed his hand. "I know you won't. If your mom's okay with us staying there, I'm all for it."

"She'll like that, she really will."

Time passed so quickly when you were in love. It seemed like only yesterday that he'd met her family, and now he was in the car headed for St. Louis with her by his side. He and Tammy were going to spend Christmas week in St. Louis. She was excited to meet his parents and hadn't stopped speaking about it since he'd invited her.

When he went to pick her up, he was surprised with the amount of luggage she had for their week's stay. "Tammy, we're not going out of the country for a month. We're only going to be gone a week. What's with all of this luggage?"

"I've got gifts for everyone."

"My family doesn't expect you to give them gifts. You're just meeting them for the first time and all."

"First impressions make a huge difference, and I want your family to like me."

"I don't think you'll have to worry about that in the least. If Gabriella loves you, they all will. She's the toughest of them all, and you passed her test with flying colors." She blushed at his comment. He raised his hand to her cheek. "You have absolutely nothing to worry about. I want you to enjoy your vacation. Remember, you're dating me, not my family."

"I realize that. I love you so much, and I don't want to disappoint you in any way."

"You could never disappoint me."

Their five-plus hour drive to St. Louis took longer than they expected. They encountered a traffic jam right outside of Bloomington, Illinois. A tractor trailer had flipped over on the side of the road. By the time they were upon the scene, medical personnel were already assisting the driver. "I think we should stop and make sure they have the situation under control."

Alejandro pulled to the side of the road and hopped out of the car. Within minutes he'd returned. "I'm glad I stopped. The driver's dazed, but the paramedics have it under control."

"Do you always stop when you come upon an accident?"

"Yeah, I do."

By the time they arrived at his parents' house, it was almost five o'clock. They'd left Madison just after seven and had stopped for a late lunch right outside of Springfield, Illinois.

Since it was Tammy's first visit to St. Louis, he took her through busy downtown so she could see the St. Louis skyline at night. The Gateway to the West, better known as the Arch, was lighted and stood proudly over the city. He knew she was in awe as they passed through downtown.

The baseball stadium where the Rivermen played was alight in holiday lights. Downtown was gorgeous this time of year. He hoped to take her about the city to visit several of the landmarks swanked with their holiday lighting and displays.

As they neared his parents' home, he pulled to the side of the road.

"Is this it?"

"No, my parents are in the next block." He reached across and ran his hand along her shoulder. "Are you ready?"

"Ready for what?" she playfully asked.

"To meet my parents?"

"Oh yeah." She chuckled and clasped his hand. "I'm more than ready." He leaned over, kissing her parted lips. "Come on, let's get this show on the road. I can't wait to meet your mom and see Gabriella."

"Don't forget the men in the family, too."

"Oh, I won't, but I don't think I'll have to impress them as much as I do your mom." She smiled at him. "And Gabriella likes me, so I don't have to worry about her."

He kissed her again and then pulled away from the curb, heading towards his parents' home. As he slowed to turn into the driveway, she was taken aback by the decorations. "Wow, look at that. They certainly know how to be festive."

"It's all my dad's doing. He loves to decorate the out-side, while mom takes care of the inside." He parked behind the third stall of the garage where he knew no one else would park. Turning to her once again, he asked, "Ready?"

"I'm more than ready. Let's go." He met her at the side of the car and started towards the front door, when the kitchen door flew open and Gabriella came bounding down the steps.

"What took you so long?"

"Traffic." Alejandro groaned as he watched his sister pull Tammy into her arms. Before he knew it, they were inside and he was surrounded by his parents in the kitchen.

"Mom, Dad, I'd like to introduce you to Tammy." He turned to her. "Tammy, my parents."

Her smile lit up the kitchen as he introduced her. "It's a pleasure meeting you, Dr. and Mrs. Alvarez."

"Honey, quit with the formalities. Call us John and Maria."

"Okay then, John and Maria, it's a pleasure."

His mom had prepared appetizers since she knew Alec and Joe wouldn't arrive for some time. The office had just closed, and they had rounds to make before they could join them.

He could tell Tammy was enjoying herself. She hadn't stopped smiling since she walked through the door. He enjoyed watching her interaction with his parents. She fit right in. Of course, Alec made his grand appearance, letting everyone know he'd arrived. He was followed a short time later by Joe.

His mom served dinner almost as soon as her other sons arrived. Joe still had to return to the hospital, and Alec's phone had rung almost non-stop through dinner. He'd been assigned to be on-call for the weekend. Groaning, he answered his sixth call since arriving. "Dad, you know when to call it, don't you? I can't believe you're on vacation, leaving all of this sickness to me."

Joe immediately chimed in. "Hey there, bro, you're not alone in this. Don't forget I'm working, too."

"I don't see your phone ringing off the hook."

"No, but I still have to return to the hospital."

Alejandro listened to his brothers go back and forth, whining about nothing. He knew they enjoyed what they did, working alongside their father.

≈

When it was time to turn in for the night, Maria showed Tammy to her room. "I've given you Gabriella's old room. It has its own bathroom."

"Thank you, Maria. I appreciate you allowing me to stay here."

"Oh honey, of course. I'm so excited to meet you. I'm glad my son has finally found someone to share his life with." Tammy raised her eyes to Maria. "Sweetheart, I can tell how much Alejandro cares about you. He's never acted this way and definitely has never brought anyone home with him since he left here to attend medical school."

Maria ran her hand along Tammy's cheek. "I think you love my son."

Tammy's face lit up. "I do, Maria, I do. I love him with all of my heart."

Maria led Tammy into Gabriella's room. Alejandro had already brought her luggage up to the room. "My goodness dear, did you pack for a month?"

She chuckled at her comment. "Alejandro asked me the same thing."

"My son travels light, so I'm sure he wasn't happy with all of this."

"He wasn't, but I explained and I think he understood."

"I'm sure Alejandro will be right up. I'll leave you

alone now."

Tammy reached for Maria's hand. "Thank you again for this. I'm so excited to share the holidays with your family."

"We're glad you're here. I'll let Alejandro fill you in on our schedule and traditions. I'm sure he'll show you around town tomorrow. Good night, dear. Sleep well." Tammy pulled Maria into a tight hug.

"Thank you again. You've been most welcoming."

"Oh dear, thank you." Maria walked from the room and headed down the stairs where she met her son along the way.

"You've got a keeper there, son. Don't ruin a good thing."

"I won't, Mom, I won't."

As he turned to enter Tammy's room, Maria added, "Son, it's good to see that smile on your face. It's been missing far too long. I like this change, Alejandro. You seem relaxed— at ease. Something I haven't seen in many years."

Tammy, who stood just inside the doorway, accidentally overheard Maria's comments. Relief filled her with a sense of knowing she'd been accepted by his mother.

Christmas at the Alvarez's was a magical time for Tammy. She hadn't known what to expect. She knew how laid back her family could be but was shocked with Alejandro's. They all attended midnight mass. It was beautiful and instantly she fell in love with the church. When she walked into the vestibule, she enjoyed the strong scent of pine that came from the fresh-cut Christmas trees that adorned not only the entrance but also the sacristy. Poinsettias flanked the steps to the altar. It was a sight she'd never forget.

Maria hurried them home as she'd planned a quick celebration after mass. She'd made several decadent desserts that Tammy could still taste the next morning. She felt like she'd just gone to bed when she was awakened by Alejandro's soft touch as he swept a kiss against her cheek. She opened her eyes to his broad smile. He seemed as happy as a kid in a candy store waiting for his special treat. She'd never seen him this excited before. He had a glimmer in his eyes when he told her he wanted to share his gift with her before breakfast.

"Can I at least get dressed?" she asked as she sat up.

"Yeah, sure, but hurry up. I can't wait a minute longer." She wasn't sure what to expect when she returned to the room. He was sprawled on her bed. Reaching out to her, he drew her into his arms and dropped a chaste kiss onto her nose. "Merry Christmas, my love," he said as he hugged her tightly. He cocked his head. "Is something wrong," he asked.

"No, why would you say that?"

"You have a funny look on your face."

"Of course, I do. You woke me from a sound sleep and expected me to get moving right away. I need a minute to wake up."

He guffawed at her as he reached into his pocket. She noticed the blue box that he'd withdrawn. Her mouth went dry, and she ran her tongue across her lips. She'd become nervous all of a sudden. She could only imagine what was in the box and why he was so excited. Was this it?

"Before you get all excited, this isn't what you may think it is, but this is something special." He slid the gift into her hand. "Open it." She chewed on her lower lip as she slipped the ribbon from the box. She opened the lid and a velvet box sat before her eyes. She hesitated before she dropped the velvet box into her hand.

She looked up at him. "Alejandro," she softly said. "What have you done?"

"I wanted to do something special for you. Please just open it." She closed her eyes as she eased the lid open. She felt his hand as it cupped the side of her face. "Open your eyes. I hope you like them."

Slowly she opened her eyes. There, sitting in the Tiffany blue jeweler's box, was the most beautiful pair of earrings she'd ever seen. They were heart shaped emeralds surrounded in diamonds.

"Something you can wear to the hospital and not have to worry about."

Her hand shook as she ran her fingers across the stones. "They're beautiful," she said as she leaned over and wrapped her arms about his neck. "Thank you so much. I love them and I love you." She ran her fingers through his hair as she kissed him soundly on the lips. "This is too much."

"Not for the woman I love."

"But Alejandro…"

"No buts. I want to see them on you. Put them in." She rushed to put the earrings in and dropped one of the backs onto the bed. It got lost in the blankets. She became flustered as she searched for it, and then she noticed the bright smile cross his face.

"Is this what you're looking for?" he asked, holding out his upturned palm.

"What do you think?" she said as she grabbed the back to her earring and put it in place. Just as she leaned in to kiss him, her stomach began to rumble. "What smells so good?"

"Breakfast," he exclaimed as he placed a kiss on her lips and reached for her hand. "Come on, let's go before Alec and Joe eat it all." She stumbled as she was getting off the bed. He grabbed her. "What's your hurry?"

"You said we needed to hurry."

"I was just kidding. Mom makes enough for an army."

They had a sumptuous and relaxing breakfast and then opened their gifts. Tammy was surprised that his parents had given her a glass ornament from the Botanical Gardens. Gabriella had given her a candle and some bath gels from her favorite store. Alec and Joe had surprised her. They'd gone in together and purchased her and Alejandro a weekend at one of the resorts in the Wisconsin Dells.

She gasped when she opened the card. Wide-eyed, she looked up at Alejandro. "Look what your brothers gave us." She didn't know what to say, she was so shocked.

"I'm sure you both will need sometime away during your long winter," Joe said as he joked about the some-times-grueling Wisconsin winters.

"It does seem to go on and on," Alejandro commented as he stood and shook both of his brothers' hands. "That was really nice of you."

"Think nothing of it," Alec declared. "You both work too hard, and we're sure you can use the time away."

The rest of the day passed in a blur, and before she knew it, it was time for them to return home. Right before leaving, Maria pulled her into her arms and whispered into her ear, "My dear, you're the reason that Alejandro is happy. You've put the smile back on his face that's been missing for so long. He loves you, and I know you love him, too."

"I do." The words softly passed her lips as she repeated, "I do, Maria— with all of my heart."

Chapter Seven

CHRISTMAS HAD BEEN A MAGICAL time for Tammy. As she sat waiting for Alejandro to pick her up for their Valentine's celebration, she found herself reliving Christmas morning and his present. She'd barely taken her earrings off since he gave them to her. She often found herself straightening them, remembering that it had been an extraordinary day. She loved his family and was sorry when the two of them had to return home. She recalled Maria's last words as though she'd just spoken them. She realized how right his mother had been as a smile seemed to always be plastered on Alejandro's face.

She hadn't heard the doorbell when it first rang. She'd been reliving one of the most special moments in her life. She became startled when he wrapped his knuckles against the window.

"Didn't you hear the bell," he asked as he walked into the foyer.

"No, I didn't. Are you sure you rang it?"

"Of course I did. I heard it…" He cocked his head at her. "I guess you were living in your fantasy world, huh?"

"You caught me," she said as she wrapped her arms around him.

"Happy Valentine's Day, my love," and with that he withdrew a bouquet of roses that he'd kept hidden behind his back.

She threw her hands in front of her face. She was totally shocked by his gesture. Even though he'd given her flowers on several occasions in the past, he still surprised her. "Alejandro, they're gorgeous." She drew them to her nose, sniffing their sweet smell. "I love the scent of roses. Thank you. No one has ever given me flowers before you did."

He still seemed surprised by that. "I'm glad to hear that I was the first. Are you ready to go?"

"Yep, just let me get my coat." She grabbed the vase of flowers and set them on the end table in the family room and reached for her coat that was lying on the sofa. He took it from her and helped her on with it. Leaning over, he kissed the nape of her neck. "In all my excitement earlier, with you not answering the door, I forgot to tell you— you look gorgeous tonight."

She turned and hugged him close. "Thank you, Alejandro. And I forgot too, Happy Valentine's Day." She kissed him. "Thank you for the beautiful flowers."

He reached for her hand and led her to the car. "Where are we going for dinner?" she asked.

"I found this little restaurant on the outskirts of town. I've heard a lot of good things about it, so I thought we'd give it a try."

They drove for what seemed like forever. *Outskirts of town? This isn't the outskirts of town. More like the next county!* She wasn't going to complain because she loved each and every minute spent with him.

When he finally pulled off the road, she was taken by surprise. It was an old grist mill that had been converted into a restaurant. It had been a warmer than usual winter and the waters in the area hadn't frozen over. The mill, in fact, seemed to still be operational as the paddle wheel still spun around, powered by the rushing water. "This is unusual," she stated as they made their way into the restaurant. "I didn't know these still existed."

"There are a few in the area, but I'm not sure that they're still functional. From what I read, they grind their own flours and such here." She grabbed onto the crook of his elbow as he escorted her into the restaurant.

They were greeted by a friendly hostess who led them to their table and presented Tammy with a long stemmed rose. "Compliments of the restaurant."

Tammy was excited. She'd received flowers twice today. "This is beautiful," she said as she fingered the petals. She gazed about the restaurant. "There's a lot of history here."

"There certainly is..." *And more to be come*, he thought.

The waiter presented the wine menu and shared the specials for the evening. Alejandro chose a white wine as he knew that was her favorite. While they waited for it to be served, he reached for her fingers. Holding them in his, he leaned over and kissed her cheek. "You look stunning tonight."

Shyly, she smiled and swept her hair across her shoulder. They waited as the waiter poured their wine. Alejandro took a sip and approved his choice. She noticed him lick his lips as he finished off his taste.

She couldn't believe that she was sitting in an historic restaurant on Valentine's Day with the man she loved. *Who'd have thought!*

"Tammy, hey, where'd you just go?"

"Sorry about that…I was thinking how lucky I am to be sitting here today with you on Valentine's Day. This time last year, I was alone at home watching some romantic comedy on television hoping one day I'd be as happy as the couple on screen."

"Well, are you?"

"Am I what?"

"As happy as the couple on television?"

Her eyes shimmered in the dimmed lighting. "I couldn't be happier." They were interrupted by their waiter one more time as he took their order. She rested her head on her palm as she listened to Alejandro place their order. She'd selected the salmon while he chose lamb.

"What are you smiling at?" he asked

"You."

"Me?"

"Yes, you. I love you so much, Alejandro. I feel like I'm living in a dream. Never would I have ever imagined I could be as happy as I am today." She leaned over and kissed him. "What we have right here and right now is more than I could have ever imagined."

"It can only get better," he said thinking of what he had planned.

⌒

A soft violin played in the background as they enjoyed their meal and the ambience of the restaurant. When it came time for dessert, he'd planned ahead.

The flowers were the first of his surprises of the evening. He knew she loved cheesecake, so he made sure it would be available as he'd formulated his second surprise.

"Look at the size of that cheesecake," she said, pointing to the couple across the room from them. "That looks fabulous. Can we get a piece?"

Alejandro motioned for the waiter to bring them their dessert. "When I saw that on the menu, I knew there was a slice in our future."

She laughed at his statement. "I'm going to run and use the restroom, I'll be right back." He stood and held her chair for her, placing a kiss on her cheek.

He nervously awaited her return. As he sat there, he realized what she'd said earlier was true for himself as well—well almost. Last year he'd been sitting alone at home. Although he wasn't watching a romantic comedy, he was celebrating the saving of a life. He'd performed a kidney transplant that morning on a teenager. He remembered saluting Jacob with a shot of bourbon. He often thought of his best friend, especially when he saved the life of a youngster. He owed his career to Jacob, and he was never far from Alejandro's thoughts.

Just then he felt her hand as it brushed his shoulder. "At least I'm not the only one lost in thought tonight." He grabbed her hand as she sat.

"I was thinking about where I was this time last year. I was home, honoring Jacob. I'd performed another lifesaving transplant on a teenager, and I was saluting him."

"He's never far from your mind, is he?"

"He isn't, but enough of that." He looked up as their cheesecakes were about to be served. If all went

according to plan, unlike last year where he'd been celebrating saving another life on this day, he hoped this
year he'd be setting the course for a new future for
himself and Tammy.

"For you, miss," the waiter said as he placed her
dessert in front of her. Alejandro grasped her hand
and held her gaze until the waiter finished setting his
cheesecake down. He didn't want her reacting too
quickly to his surprise.

He'd thought about this moment for weeks. He'd
carefully set it up in his mind, and he didn't want to
blow it. He squeezed her hand again and motioned to
her cheesecake. "That sure looks good."

"It does," she said as she reached for her fork. He
was still holding onto her hand when she spotted his
surprise. A look of complete shock crossed her face.
She gasped as she glanced from her dessert back to him
and then back again to her dessert. Tears immediately
filled her eyes. She dropped her fork onto her plate,
making a loud noise as it thunked off her plate onto
the table. She raised a trembling hand to her mouth.
And with that, their lives were about to take a new
path.

Alejandro dropped to his knee. Still holding onto
her hand, he brought it to his lips. His gaze focused
solely on her. Tears slipped from her eyes and down
her face. He reached up and did his best to brush them
aside. "Tammy, my life changed all those months ago
when we were dealing with Frederick. I'd seen you
every day for months on end, but in that one night, I
saw you in a different light. I was amazed how you
handled the situation. You were so compassionate. It
wasn't as though I'd never seen you at work before,
but for some reason it was different that night. Maybe

it was Frederick, I don't know. I remember asking you out, and I wasn't sure what your answer would be. I was pleasantly surprised when you said yes." She laughed at his comment.

"In that one moment, I felt my life forever changed. I remember when we ate in the cafeteria, and Crystal, the cashier, gave me a funny look when I paid for our meal. I realized then that I'd never paid for anyone's meal, let alone a woman's, the entire time I've been there. That made me realize I'd been living alone far too long.

"We've come so far since that night only a few short months ago. I never thought I'd fall for someone as quickly as I did with you, but here we are. I love you with all of my heart and soul. You've changed my life, and I can't go on without you in it for the rest of my life. So, Tammy Johansen, will you marry me? Will you become my life's partner? Will you become the mother of my children?"

By the time he finished his question, the floodgates had opened and she was trembling. He ran his fingertips along her brow. "Honey, what do you say? Will you?"

In an instant, she threw herself into his arms, "Yes," she said in a quivering voice. "I'll marry you." He pulled away and softly kissed her lips. He smoothed his hand along the side of her face and kissed her once again.

He reached towards her plate where sitting atop her cheesecake was his engagement ring surrounded by sweet strawberries and rich whipped cream. He grabbed his napkin, wiping off the whipped cream. Holding the ring up, he asked her again to marry him before he slid it onto her finger.

He kissed her ring and released her hand. He eased back into his chair as he watched her inspect it for the first time. The smile that crossed her lips took his breath away. She was going to be his wife. He felt like the luckiest man in the world. "So what do you think? Were you surprised?"

"How can you ask me if I was surprised? Look at me. I'm a bumbling mess." She gazed at her fingers. "This is the most beautiful ring I've ever seen." She grabbed for his hand and pulled him close. "Thank you. This has been the best, and I mean best, day of my entire life. I can't wait to spend the rest of my life with you."

The six months they were required to wait to marry in the Catholic Church passed in a blur. They wed on the anniversary of their first date. Tammy was a gorgeous bride. She chose a simple ivory colored dress that was strapless and laced up the back. It was sequined with stunning lace appliques. Alejandro dressed in a classic black tuxedo.

They had a small wedding party as she wanted everything about their ceremony to be plain and simple. Her sister Elsa, and Gabriella were her attendants, while Alec and Joe stood up for him. Less than two hundred guests attended the ceremony.

When the music began to play, Alejandro couldn't take his eyes off her as she walked down the aisle. He felt like he was the luckiest man in the world and didn't understand why it took him so long to ask her out. But then he did, and his world forever changed.

He knew she was nervous as her expression, a simple smile, was frozen on her face. Her eyes glimmered with unshed tears. Her fingers trembled, and her flowers shook in front of her. He mouthed to her that he loved her when he reached for her hand which seemed to break her trance-like smile. He, too, had tears in his eyes as she joined him at the altar.

In what seemed like a blink of an eye, they were retracing her steps down the aisle to a myriad of flashing bulbs as cameras clicked all around them. He knew they'd recited their vows, but he couldn't remember one single word that either of them spoke. He'd been consumed by her beauty the entire time.

As the photographer snapped the family photographs, Alejandro's smile never diminished. His mother took the opportunity while the photographer was changing his memory card to speak to him. "I've never seen you happier."

"Mom, this is the highlight of my entire life. I've found my partner. She makes me happy, and I'll love her for the rest of my life."

"Sweetheart, you waited a long time to find Tammy. She's the best thing that's happened to you since Jacob's death. She helped put that smile back on your face, and I'm grateful for that. I love her and I'm happy that's she's now a member of our family." She pulled him into a tight embrace. "The light that left your eyes the day Jacob died has once again returned. Tammy is the reason behind it, and I'm ever-thankful you've found love and happiness with her."

They enjoyed a more than raucous reception. He knew it had been loud, and his brothers had honored them with toasts, but other than that, he'd have to rely on the video of the day's events. One memory that he wouldn't need the videos for was his first dance with her. It would be ingrained in his memory forever. He'd pulled her into his arms, taken one look into her eyes, and knew he was home. She was his forever.

They had scheduled a little over two weeks off from the hospital for the wedding and their honeymoon. Neither of them had been to Hawaii, so that's where they decided to go. They left early Tuesday morning at what Alejandro would call the crack of dawn. It was a long flight from St. Louis, almost twelve hours with one layover. They arrived at just past noon Hawaii time, after six in the evening St. Louis time. They knew the jet lag would catch up with them, but they pushed through it and immediately began to play the role of tourists.

They settled into their suite and headed off to visit a nearby coffee plantation. Caffeine was just what they needed to combat their early wake-up call and the difference in time zones. After touring the plantation, they elected to return to their hotel where they enjoyed an early dinner. They turned in relatively early for Hawaii-time as they hoped to catch the sunrise. They'd decided they'd spend the next day lounging on the beach so they could recover from their travels across the Pacific Ocean.

Their honeymoon flashed by in a millisecond. Their last night on the island they attended a luau. They'd both been looking forward to it and knew it was something they'd always remember.

As they enjoyed their meal, Alejandro reached for her hand. "This has been *the* best vacation ever!"

"I couldn't agree more. Thank-you for making our honeymoon so special." She squeezed his hand leaned over and kissed his cheek. "I've taken a ton of pictures. I plan on chronicling everything we did— we'll have it always and will be something we can cherish."

Before either of them could say another word, the

hula dancers came out. They marveled at their routines.

During a pause in their dancing, Alejandro wrapped his arm about her shoulders and whispered, "I can't believe how they move." Shaking his head, he added, "I'm sure they keep the doctor's in business. I can only imagine some of the back injuries they sustain."

She chuckled at his comment. "Always, the doctor." She smiled at him. The dancers regaled them for almost an hour, and then all too soon, their special evening came to an end.

They meandered along the shoreline as the sun began to set on the horizon. With their arms wrapped around one another, they watched the last remnants of their magical vacation pass before their eyes as the glorious rays of the sun slipped into the darkened waters of the Pacific.

Before they knew it, they were once again at the airport waiting for their red-eye flight that would return them home to their busy careers. As they waited for their plane, they reminisced about everything they did while they were on the island. One of the highlights had been the luau they'd attended the night before. Not only did they enjoy the authentic foods, they were treated to a world-class group of hula dancers. Alejandro as he spoke about the luau couldn't wipe the smile from his face thinking about the hula dancers and how quickly they moved on stage. He was sure they'd have some type of recurring injury especially if they didn't take care while performing their dance moves.

"Ready to go home?" he asked as they boarded the plane.

"What do you think?" She had a window seat and sat while he stowed their carryon bags in the overhead bin.

With one hand on the overhead, he bowed down and smiled. "No, but I'm sure you're missing our hectic schedules." He sat down, raised the arm rest, and wrapped his arm around her. "We have to remember to make time for us — just like we did while we were dating."

"We will." She placed her hand on his knee and looked up at him. "Thank you. Thank you for a magical honeymoon. I will never, ever forget it."

"It was my pleasure." He cupped the side of her face and leaned in close. "I love you now more than the day we got married. My love for you grows by the day. You're my life, Tammy. I feel at home with you in my arms. I never, ever want to lose this feeling. You're my everything." He kissed her forehead. "We'd better try and get some sleep. This is going to be a long flight."

Just as the plane lifted off into the night sky, he wrapped his arms around her. They fell into a peaceful slumber and woke not too long before they landed in Dallas. They had a quick turnaround and then were airborne again on their final leg home.

They still had a couple of days before they returned to the hustle and bustle of their jobs to recuperate from the jet lag. They spent it together, marrying all of their things into her home. It was larger than his, and he knew it would work temporarily as they hoped to expand their family.

Chapter Eight

THEY'D BEEN MARRIED FOR ALMOST three months when Tammy told Alejandro she thought she'd come down with the flu again. Her fatigue was overwhelming. No sooner would she come home, then she was asleep. Alejandro was concerned, for she didn't show the classic signs of the flu. No fever, sore throat, or cough.

He had a scheduled day off, so while she was working, he ran to the drug store. He had an inkling she might be pregnant but wasn't totally convinced. When Tammy got home that evening, he knew they had to do something. She could barely keep her eyes open. She'd lost weight as she often missed dinner because she was sleeping.

He knew home pregnancy tests were more reliable when taken first thing in the morning, but he decided they'd give it a try. They could always retake the test.

He was anxious while she slept. Sitting on the chaise lounge in their bedroom, he attempted to catch up on his reading but his mind kept wandering to the box next to him. As soon as she woke up, he'd march her into the bathroom.

She'd napped for about two hours when he heard her sigh. He jumped up with box in hand and sat beside her. He ran his fingers along her arm, waking her fully.

"Hey there," she drowsily said. "Was I asleep long?"

"A couple of hours." He wasn't sure exactly how to present the test to her, so he just raised it in front of her face. "You need to take this."

It took a few seconds for her eyes to focus on the box. "There's no way I'm pregnant."

"Are you so sure about that? We haven't actually done anything to prevent it now, have we?" He noticed the expression on her face as she looked up at him, knowing the answer to his question. He grabbed her hand and pulled her from the bed. He led her to the bathroom and handed her the test.

"I'll wait out here." The door slowly closed before his eyes, and he knew that when it reopened, his life would again be forever changed.

Minutes later, she emerged. Her eyes were as big as saucers. Joyously, with as much energy as she could muster, she said, "I'm pregnant." Her eyes were filled with tears. "I can't believe it, but you were right. I'm pregnant."

He hauled her into his arms, kissing her with fervor. "I love you so much. I can't believe it happened so fast for us. We need to get you on some vitamins. Call your doctor and schedule a visit."

She made an appointment the next day. Alejandro was so excited, he wanted to shout it from the rooftops, but he also knew that they needed to keep it to themselves for the time being.

He was waiting for her at the doctor's office when

she walked through the door. He took one look at her, and if he hadn't already known, knew she was pregnant. She absolutely glowed.

He approached her as she checked in and clasped her hand in his. He leaned over and kissed her cheek. "You're radiant." She hadn't been able to wipe the smile from her face once she'd seen the lines on the test that proved that she was pregnant.

They had barely taken a seat when her name was called. He reached for her hand and squeezed it as they walked through the doorway. In a few short months they'd gone from two single people to a married couple and now they were expecting a child. His life's dreams were coming true.

Tammy had a textbook pregnancy with little to no morning sickness. Alejandro was with her every step of the way. He attended all of her doctor's appointments and even shed a few tears right alongside her when they had their first ultrasound. He often wondered if he were living in a dream, and he'd wake to find everything was just that— a dream.

He carried the ultrasound photo with him everywhere, and when he doubted where he was in his life, he pulled out the snapshot of his child and immediately brought himself back to the reality of the moment. He was going to become a father, and that was something he hadn't thought possible just a little over a year ago. His life had definitely changed— changed for the better, and he couldn't wait until that moment when he'd hold his child for the first time.

The calm, confident doctor was not that when he

wheeled Tammy into the hospital at three o'clock on a cool September morning. Tammy had woken him from a sound sleep to tell him she was in labor and that her water had broken. He was half asleep when he rushed out the door, dressed still in his pajamas, forgetting the most important thing— her. He was flabbergasted and his mind was all over the place as he drove them to the hospital.

"Please don't forget that I'm in the car," she groaned as a contraction hit her. He glared at her. "Well, you ran out of the house without me. Aren't I the one having your baby?"

"You are and I'm sorry about that. I guess I'm a tad bit nervous."

"Nervous? Where did you get that idea?" When they arrived at the hospital, he grabbed a wheelchair, and after checking in, they headed off to the maternity ward. She was in labor less than ten hours when she'd delivered their son, Michael Connor Alvarez, right on schedule. It was just days after their first anniversary. He was the first grandchild on both sides of the family. Maria and John drove up from St. Louis within hours of Alejandro's call to say Tammy was in labor, making it to the hospital just in the nick of time.

As he sat holding his hours-old son, he still couldn't believe the direction his life had taken. As he watched Michael move his lips as he slept, out of nowhere he thought of Jacob. He knew Jacob would be happy for him. It had taken him longer than he expected, but he now had the family he'd longed for.

Alejandro lost track of time as he lovingly watched Michael sleep. He felt a hand brush across his shoulder and looked up. Tammy leaned over smiling at them.

"Hey, where'd you go? I've been talking to you."

He stroked his finger along Michael's brow. "I was thinking."

"About what?"

"Just that you're my *everything* and that you've given me a perfect son." He secured Michael in the crook of his arm and wrapped his other around Tammy's waist— drawing her near.

"I can't wait to take you and Michael home. I want to hold you both in my arms and take in your beauty. He's beautiful— you're beautiful."

He saw the tears forming in her eyes. "I am the luckiest man in the world! I have an unbelievably wonderful wife and a handsome son."

As the tears slipped from her eyes, he reached up wiping them away. They cherished the first moments with their son.

He hadn't felt this happy since he married Tammy just a short year ago. And in that time, his love for her had grown exponentially. He didn't know what he'd ever do without her in his life. He was in a good place with her right by his side. They made a perfect team, and he knew their bond would only strengthen in the coming years.

He was grateful for little Frederick. He'd been the glue that brought them together. If the baby hadn't been his patient, he wasn't sure he'd have seen Tammy in the same light or if he would ever have asked her out. It had been their moment in time, and he was ever-thankful for Frederick.

Alejandro took time off when Michael first came home. He wanted to spend as much time as possible with his family.

Michael's first weeks at home were an anxious time for them. No one would have known Alejandro was a world-class transplant surgeon and Tammy a PICU nurse. Every little noise he made, they jumped. They were both calmer with Maria and John around. Although his parents were only able to stay a week, they made a huge difference.

"Alejandro," his father said one night, "I can't believe how nervous you are. I don't know how you could have been a pediatrician with all of this nervousness."

"It's different when it's yours."

"That's true, but I know you've been in sticky situations before, and a baby's cry shouldn't be something that sends you over the edge."

"I know, Dad. I waited so long for him, and now that he's here, I don't want to mess up."

"How can you mess up changing a diaper?" His father raised his eyebrows and looked at his son.

Alejandro chuckled. "I guess I really can't unless I forget to close it properly, and then we'll sure have a pickle of a mess."

"From experience," John said, pointing to himself, "You definitely will."

Alejandro's parents left and since Tammy's parents were unable to get time off, they were inexperienced parents all on their own. To top off everything, Michael had his days and nights mixed up. Alejandro had gone without sleep often, but a sleepless night with a baby was not the same as a sleepless night in surgery. Michael's incessant crying had the calm, cool Alejandro at wits end. It was his turn to get up with the baby, and he paced the halls, trying to soothe him. He dropped onto the couch in the family room and ran his hand up and down Michael's back. He dreamed of everything that he wanted to experience with his son. He looked forward to sharing in his firsts: his first smile, his first time sitting-up, rolling over, and his first steps.

Somewhere along the way, both he and Michael had fallen asleep, and that's where Tammy found them. Alejandro lay sprawled on the couch safely holding Michael. A noise woke him. He slowly opened his eyes, and the first thing he saw was his son sleeping securely in his arms, and then he saw the smile on her face. "What are you smiling at?"

"My husband and son. What a precious picture you two make," she said. She approached him with phone in hand. There on the screen were the loves of her life soundly sleeping. "I'm sorry I woke you. I know you had a rough night."

"You didn't."

As she ran her hand along Michael's head, a look of profound love crossed her face. That look would be engrained in his mind for all eternity. He leaned up and kissed her soundly on the lips. Looking at his son, he murmured, "Thank you. Thank you for our son and thank you for loving me." They were happier than they'd ever been. Michael had filled a spot in their hearts that neither of them knew was missing.

Time passed quickly, and before they knew it, Michael had not only smiled but was experiencing one of the firsts that Alejandro had contemplated. The one first Alejandro didn't look forward to was Michael cutting his first tooth. He was cranky and kept them both up for nights on end. Now Alejandro knew what it was like when his colleagues talked about sleepless nights and the fact that the first tooth about killed them. He was one excited father when he saw that it had finally broken through his gum.

Nightly, he did his best to come home as soon as he could. He wasn't taking parenthood for granted and was enjoying every minute of it— except for that first tooth. Michael began to crawl early, and for days on end they thought he'd take that first step.

One evening after Alejandro had experienced a particularly hard day in surgery, he and Tammy were talking in the family room, watching their son. Michael was standing in front of them holding onto her hand, playing with a toy car. The car flew out of his hand, and before both he and Tammy could react, he took that first step. Both he and Tammy anxiously watched as he stepped away from her and walked right into Alejandro's awaiting arms. Alejandro's day had gone from one filled with pain to one overflowing with joy. "Did you see that?" Alejandro said as he swept him up into his arms. The sadness that he'd been feeling just moments before had been replaced with elation. He was where he needed to be, at home with those he loved.

Life seemed to pass by at warp speed. After another exhausting day, Alejandro took refuge in his office. He ran his hand through his hair as he glanced at the calendar on his desk. It was November fifteenth. He still couldn't believe the holidays were once again upon them. It seemed just like yesterday he and Tammy married, and he was still in shock with how quickly Michael's first year passed. He chuckled as he remembered walking out of the house, leaving her sitting on their bed when she was in labor. He'd gotten to the car, took one look at himself still in his pajamas, and realized that she wasn't with him.

He'd done his best spending as much time as he could with Tammy and Michael. He wished he could find even more minutes in the day that he could be with them. He felt complete when he held his family in his arms, a feeling he never thought possible.

Even though Tammy was working part time, she'd been scheduled to work the Thanksgiving holiday. So like the first year they dated, they planned to spend the holiday with her parents and then travel to St. Louis for Christmas. Michael had yet to visit, and Alejandro was excited to take him to his hometown.

This would be an exciting Christmas with a one-year-old. He couldn't wait to see him on Christmas morning.

Thanksgiving Day didn't turn out as planned. While Tammy worked in the PICU, Alejandro had been called in to perform another kidney transplant. A five-year-old named Zebediah had been born with one kidney. He'd been in renal failure for quite some time, and they were beginning to lose all hope of finding a kidney when a miracle happened— at least for his family. Unfortunately, it hadn't ended well for another family whose young child had been killed in an early morning accident while travelling to spend Thanksgiving Day with his grandparents.

Alejandro got the call shortly after Tammy left for her shift at the hospital. He texted her about his surgery and then quickly made arrangements to drop Michael off at her parents' house. By the time Zebediah was in recovery, Tammy's shift was almost over. He headed up to the PICU and stood just inside the unit when he saw Tammy. He watched her from afar, realizing that one look at her still took his breath away. He loved her more than he ever thought possible. He was always thankful when he had a patient in PICU because he knew she'd more than likely be responsible for their care. He'd never worked with anyone who cared more deeply for her patients and their families than his wife.

She wasn't aware of his presence. No one was near, so he strolled up behind her and wrapped his arms about her waist. Leaning in he kissed her cheek. "Hi there, sweetheart," he said and pulled away. "You about ready to go?"

"My shift is almost over, but I'm not going anywhere just yet." He knew the look. She planned on staying until Zebediah was settled, and his family was comfortable. "Don't say one word, Alejandro. You know how I am, especially when one of your patients is brought in."

"Yeah, I know, and I love you for your dedication. It's going to be a little while before he hits the floor. Shall we get a bite to eat since I'm sure we'll miss dinner with your family?"

"That sounds fabulous." He watched her as she entered some information into the computer and then turned to him. "Let's eat."

By the time they made their way to the cafeteria, it was pretty empty. In fact, the hospital had been relatively quiet with only the most critical of patients remaining over the holiday. They grabbed their turkey dinners and were greeted by Crystal.

"I'm surprised to see you both here, especially on a holiday."

"Duty calls," Alejandro said over his shoulder as he led Tammy to their table.

"I feel sorry for her," Tammy said as she took a bite of her mashed potatoes. "I don't think she has a life outside of here. She's always working."

"Sounds familiar, doesn't it?" he said.

"Yeah, I guess it does."

By the time they'd finished their dinner, Zebediah had been settled into the PICU. Alejandro made sure he was stable before he and Tammy called it a night. Their quiet Thanksgiving had done an about-face on them. One family he knew was celebrating today and another was in mourning. Unfortunately, that's what came about with their professions.

Christmas vacation couldn't come soon enough for Alejandro. He'd endured one lengthy surgery after another since Zebediah's on Thanksgiving Day, and he'd been counting down the minutes until they were on their way to St. Louis. They had so many packages in the back of their SUV, several bags overflowed onto the backseat with Michael. Alejandro shut the tailgate and shook his head.

"What's wrong Alejandro? Did you forget something?" Tammy asked.

"No, and if I did where would we put it?"

She raised her hand to her mouth trying to hide her smile. Chuckling, she said, "I guess I overbought, huh?"

"You think? You know how I am about over packing."

"I didn't over pack this time."

"You mean you did the last time?"

"I guess you could say that I did…Come on now, it's

Christmas. The first that Michael will be able to really have fun with. And you know how I feel about your family. I have gifts for them, too."

He pulled her into his arms. "I was just kidding. In fact, I was contemplating if the car is large enough to bring home everything Michael will get from my family."

"If it isn't, we'll just have to get a larger one."

He raised his brows at her. "I don't think we can get a much larger SUV."

"Honey, I was just pulling your leg. We'll be fine. I promise."

Michael had a blast on Christmas morning tearing the paper off his gifts. Of course, Alejandro had to start each one, but by the last one, he knew what to do and pulled his gift from his father's hands. Alejandro roared with laughter. "I guess he knows what he's doing." Michael pulled the last strip of paper from his gift and tossed it to Alejandro. "I think he likes playing with the paper more than anything," Alejandro added as he helped Michael pull his toy car from the box.

At one point during their gift opening, he glanced over at Tammy. She was recording Michael on her phone as he opened his gifts. He winked at her and smiled. He still couldn't believe that he was married and had a son. At times like this, he almost had to pinch himself to make sure it was real.

Chapter Nine

TIME CONTINUED TO RUSH BY, and before
Alejandro knew it, Michael had celebrated his
fourth birthday. He and Tammy couldn't have been
happier. They'd been trying to have a second baby for
some time now. Alejandro knew month after month
when she didn't turn up pregnant saddened her. Con-
ceiving Michael had been so easy, and they'd begun to
wonder if there was a problem.

Tammy was still a PICU nurse working part time,
and Alejandro was busier than ever, having taken over
as director of transplant services for the university.
One promise that he'd made to himself as he moved
up the ladder at the hospital was he'd never let his job
interfere with his family. He always made time for
Michael and Tammy. They were his life.

But with Michal now a four-year-old, Alejandro
thought he and Tammy needed some alone time, just
the two of them. They hadn't taken a vacation by
themselves since their honeymoon, so he decided to
surprise her with a trip to Florida. He planned everything, including arranging for Tammy's parents to take

care of Michael while they went away.

He knew it had been a long winter, to say the least. Madison had received record snowfall on top of frigid temperatures. When he'd come up with the idea, it was his way to just get out of the cold. He'd been working long hours and wanted to spend quality time with Tammy, enjoying the warm waters of the Gulf.

He felt like he was proposing all over again. He decided to take her back to the restaurant where he proposed and surprise her with the trip. He hadn't told her where they were headed, but she figured it out. "We're going back to the grist mill, aren't we?"

"And pray tell how did you come to that conclusion?"

"I put two and two together. I remember the long drive, but I also recall it was worth it." Her voice softened. "The restaurant holds a special place in my heart. That's where my life forever changed when you proposed."

They were greeted by the same friendly hostess that seated them before. "Hi, Dr. Alvarez. Your table is ready."

He placed his hand along her back as he guided her to their magical table. For once she was speechless. Alejandro watched as she raised her quivering hand to her mouth. There sitting in the middle of the table was a dozen roses in a crystal vase. He pulled out her chair and as she sat kissed the top of her head.

"You did this for me?"

"Of course, I did. I wanted this to be a special evening." A few moments passed as they waited for the waiter to bring the wine Alejandro had previously selected.

Out of the corner of his eye, he watched Tammy as

their wine was poured. Her smile lit up the room.

"To us," he said as he raised his glass. And then, he reached into the inside pocket of his suitcoat withdrawing a plain white envelope.

"For me?"

He nodded his head smiling brightly at her. He couldn't wait for her to open his surprise.

She slid open the seal and withdrew the contents.

He rested his head in his palm watching her closely—waiting for the moment when she realized what sat in front of her.

She could hardly speak when she grasped what she held in her hand—plane tickets and a hotel reservation. "I can't believe you did this." She cried as he ran his fingertip along her cheek. "I need this; no, we need this." She wiped the tears from her face. "I love Michael, but I think we deserve some alone time too."

"That's why I did it. It's been a long winter, and I think we owe it to ourselves to get out of the city and enjoy the sun for a few days."

They flew into Miami and drove down to Key West, Florida He'd arranged for a house right on the beach. They spent the first day in bed, something they hadn't been able to do since before Michael's birth. They walked on the beach and enjoyed the magnificent sunsets that the area was known for. Tammy even agreed to go deep sea fishing, something Alejandro had wanted to do for a long time.

Alejandro stood along the railing of the boat with his reel in the water. They'd been on the boat in the hot sun for more than two hours.

"I can't believe I joined you on this boat! You haven't even had a bite. Look at all of the beach time I've missed."

He quirked his brow at her knowing well enough that she was joking. She never complained. He believed she was bored more than anything. And then, he felt it— a hard tug on his pole. Thankfully he'd had a strong grip on it or it would have flown out of his hands.

"Oh wow! I've got something." Alejandro yanked on his pole and wound the reel. He fought and fought the fish all the while Tammy stood by his side cheering him along.

"Alejandro, you can do it. Reel it in," she yelled at his side.

As he worked furiously to bring his fish in, Tammy stood by his side jumping up and down with excitement.

He could hear her clicking away on her camera as he hauled the huge fish over the side of the boat.

"You did it!"

"Yep, I did! See what you would have missed if you were sunning on the beach."

"I was only joking."

"I know that."

By the time he finished pulling the fish onboard, it was time for the boat to return to port. What had started as a non-descript day turned into one filled with excitement as they stowed the fish. As the wind whipped through their hair, Alejandro leaned down and brushed his lips across hers. "Thanks for putting up with this."

"I had fun. I really did watching you reel in the fish. Another memory for me to add to our scrapbooks."

She handed her camera to one of the captains as he took their picture with Alejandro's trophy fish.

Before they knew it, their time was up, and they were flying home back to the cold Wisconsin winter.

It seemed winter would never fade, but finally, spring arrived. Along with it came the day Alejandro had dreamed of for eons. Michael was old enough to play T-ball, and Alejandro was almost giddy with excitement when he stood in line to sign him up. It felt like Christmas all over again as a kid, except this time it was he who was filling out forms and getting Michael's team shirt. He couldn't wipe the smile off his face, especially when he presented the team shirt to his son.

As soon as Michael had been able to hold a bat in his hands, Alejandro had him standing in front of a tee, practicing. He worked with him all the time and loved watching him concentrate as he tried to smack the ball off of the tee. Both of them were over the top excited. Alejandro had wanted to be his coach but knew with his schedule he wouldn't be able to commit to all of the practices and games, so instead, he volunteered to help out when he could. On top of this milestone, in just two short years, Michael would be old enough to join Cub Scouts. Alejandro couldn't wait because scouting had taught him so many life skills. Both he and Jacob had gone through the program. They'd become Eagle Scouts, and he knew that the award helped him. It would benefit Michael as he sought to further educate himself and seek employment.

With spring came not only T-ball, but the rains. Rivers were swollen after the snow melt, and with the heavy downpours to the already soggy ground, flooding was imminent. The team hadn't been able to play one game, yet. They'd held a few practices, but then the rains came, and the playing fields were surrounded by water. Michael was disappointed and so was Alejandro. The opening game had to be cancelled, but the weather forecast for the following week looked promising, and Alejandro was relieved. He took his phone and showed Michael the forecast that the following week was all filled with smiling suns.

"Dad, does that mean we'll be able to play?" Michael asked.

"Fingers crossed, it does."

Tammy hadn't felt well for several days. She'd been nauseous. Thinking she'd picked-up a bug from Michael, she'd tried her best to weather the storm, but Alejandro had finally had enough. It took him having a stern conversation with her to schedule a doctor's appointment. "You don't want to miss Michael's first T-ball game, do you? If you're sick, you won't be able to go."

"Mom, you can't miss my first game *ever*. Dad showed me the smiling suns on his phone, and I know we'll play next week."

"Okay, I'll make the appointment, but Michael, you're going to have to go with me."

"That's fine, Mom. I just want you well for my game."

Alejandro watched her pull him into her arms. He knew she wasn't feeling well, but you could never tell by the smile that spread across her face. He knew how much she loved their son.

⁓

Tammy phoned her doctor and was able to capitalize on a cancellation the very next day. Alejandro had an opening in his schedule, so they decided she'd drop Michael off at her parents, and Alejandro would meet her at her doctor's office. He was concerned about her, but he didn't want her to know how worried he truly was.

She was just getting ready to leave the house when Alejandro texted her. *I've just been called into surgery. Sorry, I won't be able to make your appointment.* A kidney had become available for one of his patients, and he had to act on it immediately. When she got his text, she decided to take Michael with her to the doctor. She phoned his office unsure if he was still available.

"Sorry, Tammy, but he just went into surgery," his assistant informed her.

"I just got his text a few moments ago Mirabelle and thought I might catch him before he went into the OR. Let him know that I'm taking Michael with me to my appointment instead of dropping him off at my parents. They live so far out with the rain and all…"

"Okay, I will. Stay safe."

Tammy understood that Alejandro needed to be in surgery, so she packed up Michael and they weathered the fierce downpour as they drove to her doctor's office.

She knew Alejandro was bothered that he couldn't attend her appointment. His patient was important to him, but so was she. Tammy knew she meant the world to him, and wasn't surprised that right before he went into surgery he sent her another quick text message. *I wish I could be there with you— let me know as soon as you know what's up. Love you.* Tammy was a mess as she drove to the doctor's office. She'd barely been able to see the road through the torrents of rain and at one point had barely been able to stop at a stop sign. She'd applied her brakes and her tires hydroplaned across the roadway, barely coming to a stop. White knuckled, she continued on and sighed loudly when she saw the entrance to the medical facility. *We made it.* They'd made it safely, albeit she wasn't sure how.

She'd received his message right as she pulled into the parking lot and replied back. *I'm here. Roads are a mess! Flooding all about. I'll call you as soon as I get home. Love you, too.*

Alejandro's surgery went a little longer than he expected, and by the time he got back to his office it was almost five. Tammy's appointment had been at two. He grabbed his phone, expecting to see her message but there was none. The last text was when she arrived at the doctor's office.

He was concerned. It wasn't like her to not check in, especially when she knew he was expecting her to. He phoned home and there was no answer. He dialed her cell, and it went directly to voicemail. He left a quick message, wondering where she was.

Alejandro checked on his patient one last time before heading home. He once again checked his cell, and there still wasn't a message from her. He was worried. He tried her cell and their home again, and both phones went to voicemail.

As he made his way to his car, he realized that with the area flooding, maybe the phone lines were down. He jumped into his car and started home. The rain was pounding against his windshield. He could hardly see the road. As he neared the turnoff to his home, the rain lessened and he could see the standing water on both sides of the road. The farmland was flooded and rivers of water ran through them. He contemplated pulling over, but he needed to get home. Home to his family.

As he pulled up to the house, he noticed there wasn't a light on. He thought it strange since the neighborhood was lit up like a Christmas tree. He tried the garage door opener, and the door opened just fine. But Tammy's car wasn't parked in its usual space. In fact, he didn't see it anywhere. It wasn't in front of the house, and it definitely wasn't in the driveway.

A sense of fear overcame him. He dashed inside and frantically called for her, for Michael. No answer. He raced from room to room, thinking maybe she'd fallen asleep. No Tammy. His heart beat wildly against his chest. *Where were they?*

He tried her phone again, no answer. The always calm, cool, collected Alejandro was frantic with worry. He began to pace the kitchen wondering where they could be. He phoned her parents, and they hadn't heard from her. He was out of options. He didn't know what to do next.

It was still pouring rain when he heard the doorbell ring. He ran to the door, praying it was Tammy who'd just forgotten her key. He threw open the door and in that moment he had his answer— one that would forever change his life.

Alejandro took one look at his visitor and knew. He turned, trying to put as much distance as possible between him and the police officer. In the process, he stumbled backwards, landing hard against the newel post that led upstairs. He slumped to the steps. He swept his hands through his hair, trying not to listen to the words that were being spoken to him. If he couldn't hear them, then whatever was being said couldn't be possibly true.

"Dr. Alvarez?"

He couldn't make eye contact, he just couldn't. His world was crumbling right before his eyes. He felt the tears gliding down his face and then became aware of the dark blue coat, the hand resting on his arm. He felt the blood rushing through his head. He couldn't concentrate on the words that were being spoken because they couldn't be true. He knew he needed to acknowledge what the officer was saying, but he couldn't. His brain wouldn't allow him to hear what was being said. "Take a deep breath, sir."

Alejandro couldn't focus. He leaned over his knees and took one deep breath after another. His mind raced. *It can't be true.* The only words that he could mutter over and over again were, "No, no. It can't be..."

He felt the officer at his side for some time and then raised his eyes to him. "My wife and s-son— what happened? Where are they?"

Alejandro rested his elbows on his knees and his hands in praying motion against his chin.

"Dr. Alvarez, your wife was driving along Highway 113. From what we can gather, a mini flash flood came out of nowhere. It swept her car into the trench alongside the Sunnyside Farm, and it flipped over. By the time we arrived, the car was filled with water. She and your son drowned at the scene. There was nothing we could do."

He screamed their names at the top of his lungs. Tears stung his eyes and fell over his fingertips, drenching the floor in front of him.

"Is there someone we can call for you?"

Alejandro sat in an absolute fog. He couldn't believe what he'd just heard. Tammy was gone...Michael was gone…His life would never be the same. Alejandro's phone lay on the steps beside him. He'd dropped it when he'd collapsed. It began to ring. He was in another place, another time, and couldn't connect the ringing sound to his phone. It was just noise filtering into his ears.

The officer reached for his phone and answered. "Hello."

"Alejandro?"

"Ah no, please hold a moment." The officer handed him the phone. Alejandro was in a state of shock and could barely say hello. He didn't think to check the caller.

"Alejandro, is someone there?" He heard his mother's voice, and the dam broke even further.

He cried out in agony. "Mom?"

"Alejandro? What's the matter? Who was that man who answered your phone? Are you alright?"

"No, I'm not. I'll never be the same again."

"What's wrong?" she pleaded. "Tell me Alejandro, what's happened?"

"She's dead."

"Who's dead?"

"Tammy."

"Tammy's dead? How can that be?" his mother asked on deaf ears.

"…And so is my son. Michael's dead, too." Upon uttering those words, he felt a pain ratchet through his chest as though he were stabbed directly in the heart. Alejandro dropped the phone and rolled himself into a ball, openly crying for the woman he loved more than life itself and for his son who never had a chance to experience life.

Chapter Ten

THE NEXT FEW DAYS PASSED in a whirlwind. Only hours after discovering Tammy's death, he found himself wrapped in his mother's arms. The strong, confident man had fallen completely to pieces.

After he'd dropped the phone in utter despair, Maria had spoken with the officer. She instructed him how to contact Tammy's family, then, while she contacted Joe, Alec, and Gabriella, John made plane reservations. Luck had been on their side, and a plane was scheduled to leave for Madison in the next couple of hours. Maria didn't know how she did it, but she packed in a complete fog.

Gabriella had been beside herself. She wasn't able to fly out immediately because she needed to make arrangements for someone to take over her classroom. She would leave later in the day. Alec and Joe would join them as soon as they could arrange for another clinic to cover their calls. This was a tragedy, and they knew their peers would step up and cover the practice while they were gone.

Maria took one look at her son as she pulled away

from him. She couldn't believe her eyes. Her son had aged so in the last few hours. She'd just seen a picture of him with Tammy holding up a grouper that he'd proudly caught off Key West. He'd looked so happy, tanned, and so in love. The smile that spread across his face was priceless. And the look of love that he'd had in his eyes for Tammy was one she'd never ever forget.

Now as she gazed at her son, she witnessed the antithesis of that photograph. His eyes were puffy and red-rimmed, and dark circles surrounded them. He was on the pale side, and his face was drawn with the sadness that was consuming him. He looked completely lost and totally devastated.

She wanted to cry herself but somehow held her tears at bay. She led him into the family room where Tammy's parents were. John was quietly speaking with Mark. As they entered, she noticed Phyllis holding a tray containing a coffee carafe. Maria approached her as she set the tray down and pulled her into her arms. "I'm so, so sorry, Phyllis."

Maria watched as she poured a cup of coffee, handing it to her husband. "Coffee?" she asked Maria as she began to pour another cup. Maria was amazed with how well Tammy's parents seemed to be holding up. She imagined they were still in a state of shock.

Her son slumped onto the settee. She joined him and reached for his hand, holding it tightly like a mother would a frightened child's. She gazed at him. He was lost in a completely different world, a different time, as he gazed into the distance. She knew he wasn't truly aware of her presence. He was in shock, and she prayed that he would come around. It had only been a few hours since their deaths and, for the first time since he'd been a small child, she was truly worried about her son. In his entire life, she'd never seen him like this. He was adrift.

Out of the blue, he jumped from the couch, grabbed his cell phone and hurried towards the door. "Alejandro, where are you going?"

"To the hospital. I have a patient I must see."

"But Alejandro…" Her words fell on deaf ears as he ran from the house.

"Let him go," John said as they heard the garage door raise, and he drove out the driveway. All four of them watched as his car disappeared from sight.

"He's hardly spoken a word," Mark said as they stood there.

Maria grabbed ahold of John and listened as Mark filled them in on the missing pieces. "She'd been returning from a doctor's appointment and was swept away in a flash flood. By the time the emergency personnel got there, they were already gone."

Maria gasped. Her heart bled for her son. He'd waited years to meet the woman of his dreams, the love of his life, and then she was gone in an instant. No forewarning. Nothing could have prevented the accident except her not venturing out in the storm.

Gabriella, Alec, and Joe joined the family the next day. Gabriella's flight had been delayed the previous day. Upon her arrival, she sought out Alejandro. She knew he was a mess, and she was going to do everything in her power to help him overcome his loss. She'd already arranged a leave of absence from her job. She would do absolutely anything she could to help her brother weather this storm as she knew it would be awhile before he regained himself. He'd lost his best friend—the love of his life—and his son all in one moment in time. It would take longer than any of them could imagine for him to recover, if he ever did.

Gabriella approached Alejandro and pulled him into her arms. Immediately, she saw the faraway look in his eyes. She was worried more than she let on as she led him to a nearby couch. She sat beside him and did her best to let him talk. It was just the two of them as Tammy's parents had gone home, and their parents had gone grocery shopping. Alec and Joe had wandered off somewhere, giving her the time she needed to speak with him.

They had a special bond that was unbreakable. If anyone could get him to open up, it would be her. She let him be, praying he would talk, but he didn't. He sat, staring straight ahead. They were interrupted by her parents' return. Alejandro jumped up from the couch and met them in the kitchen. The one moment where she'd hoped to get him to open up had gone. She'd give him the time he needed. The loss was still so new to all of them. She prayed in time he'd seek her out and share his thoughts.

The time leading up to the funeral passed all too quickly. At the wake, he stood the entire time between their two caskets and hardly said a word. He spoke only when spoken to. Alejandro grew more despondent as time passed.

At the funeral, he sat stoically. From the time he entered the church, the expression on his face never altered. He sat ramrod straight, face forward, eyes never once leaving the caskets. Gabriella sat beside him holding his hand— using it as her own lifeline. She leaned into him, laying her head against his shoul-

der while Max spoke proudly of his sister. Alec spoke
on behalf of their family. In a somber tone, he thanked
the Johansens for their daughter and said how she'd
been a breath of fresh air when she joined their family.
At one point, Gabriella looked up at Alejandro as he
fought back tears. She was proud of him as he seemed
to be holding it together as best as he could.

Her parents and brothers returned to St. Louis while
she remained with Alejandro. He'd wanted to return
to work, but she convinced him to stay home a few
days longer. She feared if he returned to work too
soon, he'd immerse himself in the hospital. She knew
he needed to take some time to himself and learn to
live again without Tammy and Michael by his side.

A few days after the funeral, Gabriella happened
to catch him staring at his phone. Tears were gliding
down his face. She walked up beside him and noticed
he was looking at the weather forecast. She thought
he was having a moment but didn't realize the under-
lying meaning behind it. Seven smiling suns stared
back at him. She knew by the look on his face that
he'd been thrust back in time.

She placed her hand on his arm. "Is everything
okay?"

He pointed to his phone. "Seven smiling suns," he
said.

Smiling at him she said, "Great weather forecast. We
sure need it." She saw the light dim even further from
his eyes as he softly spoke.

"The last time I saw that on my phone we were
hoping for good weather so Michael could play his
first t-ball game. I'll always remember him asking me,
'Does that mean we'll be able to play?'"

She could only imagine that that conversation was

on constant replay in his mind. She watched him closely as he placed his hands over his ears as if trying to turn off his son's voice. Gabriella knew she needed to do something, so she asked him one simple question, "Can we go for ice cream? I'm starved."

For some reason that was the question he needed as he glanced up into her smiling face and nodded. "That sounds like a great idea."

After they returned from their ice cream run, Alejandro seemed more at peace. She didn't know what caused it, but she was glad. The remainder of her stay she did anything she could to help him, from going through Tammy's and Michael's things in preparation for donation to a local charity, to just sitting beside her brother listening to him recount his memories.

The day finally arrived for Gabriella to return home. She dreaded it; she feared how Alejandro would fare all alone. As she made her way to the passenger security point at the airport, she turned to Alejandro. "I'm going to check on you every day, so don't be surprised."

"I would be worried if I didn't hear from you."

"Promise me something."

"Okay."

"I want you to promise me that no matter the time of day if you need to talk, call me. I'll always be there for you, Alejandro. You're not alone." He nodded his head. "Remember, we're all here for you. Don't do this on your own."

"I hear what you're saying, and I promise to call." Alejandro hugged her closely and kissed her one last time. He watched as she proceeded through security, waving one last time as she made her way down the corridor.

As he turned his back and headed out of the terminal, he realized, for the first time in five long years, he was basically alone. He had no one to go home to and no one to truly confide in. Yes, he had his family and Tammy's as well, but it wasn't the same. She had known him inside and out. Known when he was having a stellar day or a horrendous one. He didn't have anyone outside of his peers to discuss his patients with. He didn't have her objective take on a situation, and he didn't have her beside him to get through the losses. He wasn't sure how he would survive. He looked down at the pavement as he walked. *One step at a time. I'm going to survive—one step at a time.*

Alejandro was hanging on by a thread, and he'd reached his limit. He ran his hand through his hair as he lay on the couch in his office. The hospital had become his safe haven these last few months. He rarely went home. Too many memories. He barely slept as his dreams were filled of that night.

He'd drifted off to sleep as strong storms passed overhead. The thunder rocked his office.

Realizing the doorbell had rung, he answered it. Standing before him was an officer dressed in a dark overcoat. "Dr. Alvarez?"

"Yes?" He knew his life would never be the same when he opened the door. The officer shared with him the grim news that he feared. He relived his words: Tammy and Michael were on their way home. Out of nowhere, on a stretch of open road, her car was violently swept away by rushing flood

waters. There was nothing she could do. Her car had flipped over and she and Michael had drowned before they could be rescued.

Nightly he had the same dream, always remembering how he staggered to the stairs, collapsing in shock. In the weeks that had passed since that awful night, everything was a blur. His family had come to support him, and Gabriella had been there for him, helping him pack away the memories.

He'd lost an abundance of weight. He knew his friends and colleagues were worried about him. He'd taken time off after the accident— spending much of it locked away with their memories. He couldn't remember how he learned about her doctor's appointment. He often dreamed that he'd been with her that day when she learned they were expecting their second child— a child that had most likely been conceived on their vacation.

Another round of thunder shook him. He lay there listening for what he didn't know. The peace and quiet he'd only recently sought was overwhelming him. He spun around on the couch and started to stand when he lost his balance, falling hard against a table. When he finally got his bearings, he made his way to his desk. His eyes caught their picture— a picture that had sat on his desk for several years. It had been taken at the corn maze just after they'd successfully made their way through. Tammy's eyes were bright with happiness as she'd looked up at him. He'd had his arms wrapped around her. He was happier than he'd ever been that day, outside of their wedding and Michael's birth. So many memories…He didn't think he'd ever feel that way again. Tammy had been his everything, and he was surrounded by her everywhere he went.

Every corner he turned in the hospital, he found himself looking for her. The first time he'd had to visit a patient in the PICU after her death about killed him. He'd turned the corner expecting to see her when he realized the figure standing at the desk wasn't her. She'd never greet him again when he entered the unit. He'd been overwhelmed with emotion and ducked into a conference room. It had taken him more than fifteen minutes to calm himself before he could enter the unit.

As he'd passed the desk she often sat at, he broke out into a cold sweat, and his heart beat so fast, he gasped for breath and started to tremble. One of his peers noticed him and swept him into the employee lounge. He'd thrust a cold bottle of water into his hand and made him take another moment. His colleague offered to cover for him, but Alejandro wouldn't accept it. He'd needed to overcome his grief or else he'd never be able to treat another pediatric patient at the UW. Somehow he'd gotten through that first day back in the PICU. He wasn't sure how, but he had.

He often tried to avoid the cafeteria because there were too many memories there as well. When he was forced to use it, he'd catch the look of sadness on Crystal's face when she checked him out. He always tried to smile at her, but he knew she was aware of his reluctance to be there.

He held the picture in his hands, remembering those happy days once more then he opened his desk drawer and slid their picture inside.

Alejandro knew he needed to make a change. He was on a downward spiral, and he had to get control of his life before something happened. In that moment, he knew he needed to abandon the town that had meant so much to him. He'd been in Madison since leaving for college. Almost twenty years was going to be hard to turn his back on, but he knew something must change before he ruined the accomplished career that he'd worked so hard to achieve.

His mind whirled. It was almost three in the morning. He wasn't going home, and he was as wide awake as he could be. He opened his personal email program and glanced at the screen. His eye caught Gabriella's name. She'd sent him a message near midnight.

He knew what her email was about. She'd kept her promise and emailed him daily, constantly checking on him, making sure that he'd survived another day. She was worse than his mother, making sure he slept and ate. He was haggard, and he knew that she worried he was going to fall back into that trap again.

A few short weeks after Tammy's death, Alejandro had collapsed from exhaustion. He hadn't slept or eaten for days. Even though Gabriella had constantly harassed him, he hadn't listened to her and paid the price.

She had done her best to nurse him back to health before he returned to work, making sure he ate and slept. Gabriella left believing he was stable and in a relatively good place. He survived for a few weeks after her departure, and that's when he started living in his office.

He reread her last several emails and realized that he'd missed so much of his sister's life. He'd moved away when she was still in school and had rarely gone home. His parents were getting older. His father was contemplating retirement and turning the practice over to Alec and Joe.

In that moment, he knew what he needed to do.

He wanted to get to know his family again. Twenty years was a long time of missing out on firsts and family events. He didn't have anything keeping him in Wisconsin any longer. His family was in St. Louis and that's where he needed to be.

Alejandro recalled receiving an email several months earlier. A position had opened up in St. Louis to run the Transplant Services for the local hospital. He wondered if the position had been filled. He located the email and crafted a response, hitting send before he could think about it a second time.

Epilogue

IT WAS A SUNNY DAY as he took one last walk about the house. The movers were finishing up loading the last of the boxes and furniture. That morning he'd taken his last stroll through the hospital corridors. He visited the PICU where he said his goodbyes to the staff that had meant so much to both him and Tammy. The PICU was one of the hardest places that he'd visited since her death. His mind was constantly flooded with memories of Frederick and all the time he and Tammy spent together taking care of the many families their lives had impacted.

He stood in Michael's bedroom, gazing at the murals Tammy had painted on the walls. He was going to miss this room and all of the memories he had of watching Michael sleep. He'd loved sitting on the edge of his bed. He'd watch him breathe in and out and dream of everything he wanted to do with him, from baseball to scouts to all of his firsts. He'd never be able to look at another weather forecast that was filled with smiling suns and not think of his son and all that was lost. He grasped the doorknob and slowly closed the door—

closed the door on dreams that would never come to fruition.

He entered their bedroom and ran his hand along the windowsill next to where Tammy's chaise lounge once sat. He loved that bedroom. It had been their special place where they'd lie in bed and dream of their lifetime together. His eyes moved to the spot their bed once sat. Here she'd felt Michael's first flutters of life when she'd been pregnant. He could still see the look on her face. She was astonished by what she'd felt and had immediately reached for his hand so she could share the moment with him. So many memories....

He made his way to the kitchen, recalling their first meal there and how they'd fallen in love so quickly. He was still amazed with how fast she'd captured his heart once he'd decided to ask her out.

As Alejandro stood staring out the kitchen window, he knew he'd made the right decision. Since that night when he'd decided to return to St. Louis, he'd felt a sense of calm that he hadn't felt since the morning of that unforgettable day. He knew Tammy would accept his need to leave the city that had meant so much to both of them. She would want him to find himself again and not dwell on the tragedy he'd faced.

His thoughts were interrupted. "Dr. Alvarez, we're all done here."

"Thanks," he said. "I'm going to finish my walk through. I guess I'll see you tomorrow in St. Louis." He'd purchased a home in rural St. Louis County not too far from his parents' home but far enough outside of the city that he could find peace. He'd been used to the farming community he lived in here and wanted to feel that openness when he moved.

He closed his eyes, hoping to feel her presence one

last time before closing the door on their life.

Alejandro knew he needed to find himself again. He'd have his family surrounding him, helping him get through each day without his son that had meant the world to him and without the love of his life. He'd get to know his sister all over again. He needed to be the big brother that she'd missed for so many years.

Alejandro approached the foyer. He reached for the door and opened it. Once again, he was hit with the memory of that unforgettable night. He took a deep breath. He must walk through the door one last time and close it on that part of his life.

He turned the doorknob and glanced back. In his imagination, he swore he heard Tammy's voice. He shook his head. "Goodbye, my love," he whispered as he closed the door. "You'll forever be in my heart."

He started down the sidewalk one last time. He slowly eased into his car. He started the engine and put the transmission into drive. As he released the brake and started to move forward, he knew he'd made the right decision. Tammy had changed his life in so many ways. She taught him how to love, had given him the perfect son, but she'd also forced him to grieve.

He'd never forget the love of his life. He'd mourn her and Michael until his last breath. But this change would be the best thing for him. He was starting over with a new job, a new home, and a new lease on life.

He'd made a solemn vow to himself. He'd always remember the life they had together. She'd be in his heart until the day he died. His life was forever changed by Tammy Johansen, and although he was closing the door on this chapter, she'd never be far from his thoughts. He'd always love her and knew he could never find a love like theirs again. He was going to give his life a second chance and do his best to always honor hers and Michael's memories.

IF YOU ENJOYED READING LIFE'S Forever Changed, follow Alejandro's journey as he returns to St. Louis and discovers whether he can overcome his past for a second chance at love.

Here's a sneak peek at the synopsis and first two chapters of Life's Second Chances: Book 1 in The Show Me Series.

Life's
SECOND
CHANCES

The Show Me Series

BOOK 1

Anne Stone

ANGELINA SAMUELS HAS LOST THE only job she's ever held. A last minute interview lands her a new teaching job just days before the school year is about to begin. It turns out to be the best thing that could have happened when she realizes that her best friend from college, Gabriella Alvarez, is also a member of the teaching staff.

Gabriella's brother, Alejandro, relocates to his hometown after having lived away from family and friends since he left for college to become a renowned transplant surgeon. He's settling into a new job, reacquainting himself with family and friends, and is learning to deal ever-so-slowly with the personal loss that forever changed his life.

When Angelina's sister experiences a health crisis, Alejandro is there to support her and her family. And when Angelina herself experiences a personal tragedy, Alejandro is the only one to guide her through it. As love stares down at them, can Angelina help Alejandro take that second chance on love and marriage?

Chapter One

"YOU'RE HIRED," SAID MARY FLYNN, Principal of St. Margaret's Catholic School.

Angelina Samuels couldn't believe her ears. This was her last hope that she'd find a job before the beginning of the school year—she thought she'd end up being an aide or substitute teacher. The previous school where she'd worked since graduating from college eight years ago had closed due to decreasing enrollment. She'd wanted to teach in the Catholic schools, but it was difficult finding a job with limited positions available. She was lucky that the teacher she was replacing decided to relocate unexpectedly. With her résumé on file with the school office, she had been immediately contacted to interview for the position.

"Mary, could you show me to my classroom? I've got a lot of work ahead of me to be ready by next week. Oh, by the way, what time do the meetings start tomorrow?"

"The building opens at seven, and the opening meetings begin promptly at nine o'clock." Mary stood and came around her desk to welcome her. "Welcome to St. Margaret's, Angelina. I am excited for you to join our team. I think you'll find everyone here very friendly and welcoming. I'm sure you'll fit in without any problems." Mary smiled warmly and shook Angelina's hand. "Now, let me show you to your new home-away-from-home."

Mary led Angelina from her office. Just as they turned the corner to head down a long hallway, a body came out of nowhere, flying around the corner, running smack into Angelina. Angelina blinked once, then twice, taking in the beautiful brown-haired woman who nearly knocked her off her feet. A look of utter surprise crossed the other woman's face as Angelina stood staring at her in complete shock.

Overjoyed with excitement, Angelina screamed out Gabriella's name in delight, pulling her into a tight embrace. Both women were jumping up and down in glee. Mary looked on, not sure what was transpiring before her eyes. All she knew was that two of her teachers were more than excited to see one another.

"I take it you two know one another," Mary said, laughing.

"Yes," they said in unison, continuing their dance.

"We went to college together. I lost track of you after graduation," said Gabriella, turning back to Angelina. "What happened to you? Are you taking Lauren's place since she decided to bolt before the school year?"

"Yes, I am. Mary just hired me and she was in the process of showing me to my classroom."

"Mary, don't bother. I'll take Angelina to her classroom since it is right across the hall from mine."

Mary waved them on, and arm in arm they walked down the hallway.

"I didn't know you were interviewing for the job. I

guess it came up pretty fast. When Lauren didn't show up to begin working in her classroom, Mary contacted her and discovered she was relocating and had no plans to notify her. She was a new teacher last year and had some discipline issues. I can't believe she wasn't going to let Mary know, but I guess that show's her immaturity."

"Well, I got a call from Mary this morning, and she asked me to come in this afternoon to interview. I'm stunned. I can't believe that she hired me right on the spot. I was getting a little nervous since I hadn't found a full-time job yet. I thought I was going to have to settle on being an aide or a substitute. I'd taught at St. Mark's since I graduated, but they closed at the end of the school year due to decreasing enrollment."

They stopped midway down the hallway while Angelina told her about St. Mark's closure. "I was so upset when we discovered that St. Mark's was closing. The school was over ninety years old and was so entrenched in the neighborhood. It was sad watching the enrollment decrease over the years. We saw the closure coming, but still it was difficult. Everyone wants to live in the suburbs today and people with school aged children have dwindled in the neighborhood over the years. I think I heard that the average age in the parish is something like fifty years old. I'm just really sad to see what was once a thriving school close its doors."

"Angelina, I'm just beside myself. I can't believe you are standing right here in front of me." Gabriella pulled her in for another hug. "We are so lucky to have you join the staff. You are going to absolutely love Mary. She is a one-of-a-kind principal, and she's so supportive of her teachers and staff. I'm lucky that she hired me right out of school. She's been a terrific role model to me, and I don't plan on ever leaving as long as she is here. Now, let's get you to your classroom. You're right across the hall from me. I've already finished setting up my room, so why don't I help you set up yours?"

"Would you? First of all, I need to check out the space and look at the class listing."

"You've got a lot to do to get ready for next week."

"I know I do. I'm not sure what I need, but with your help I'm sure it will take no time."

Gabriella led Angelina down the hallway to her classroom. She stopped outside the only room with a closed door. "Ready to see your new home?"

"Of course, I am! I can't wait. This day has been so surreal. Open the door already," Angelina called out. Gabriella threw open the door to Angelina's new home. She couldn't believe her eyes as she walked through the door. The room was huge! One whole wall was lined with windows that provided the best natural light she'd ever seen in any of the classrooms that she'd ever taught in at St. Mark's.

"Oh, my gosh! I love all of the light. It's fabulous."

"Yes, we're lucky. All of the classrooms have an abundance of natural light."

Angelina walked towards the back of the room and noticed the huge walk-in closet.

"Oh, my."

"What?" asked Gabriella.

"Look at all of this storage. I'm speechless, absolutely speechless."

"Now, that you've come down from this shock of a classroom, let's see what you need." They worked well into the early evening sorting through the books and materials that were in the classroom. Angelina made lists as she went of the additional materials that she would need to purchase to get her classroom together before school started the following week. She was switching grades and wouldn't be able to use anything that she had used previously. They stopped and took a break so Angelina could purchase some supplies and then returned to begin the task of preparing her classroom for the start of school.

While they were working on her bulletin boards, Angelina discovered that Gabriella lived just down the street from St. Margaret's. "I love this neighborhood. It's so family-oriented. Families are constantly milling about, taking walks, dining at the local restaurants. It can be both positive and negative living and working in the same community, but I love it and have absolutely no complaints. I love going to the grocery store and running into my students. I can't say it enough that this is a great area to live and work in."

"I'm looking forward to getting to know the neighborhood as well, along with the families. I had the same sense of neighborhood and family while working at St. Mark's. Even though I still live at home, I was able to experience those same feelings because I spent an awful lot of time in the neighborhood going to sporting events and various other parish activities. Did you move here right after school?"

"No, I lived at home for a couple of years so I could save enough money for a down payment on my house. I can't wait for you to come over and see it. It's not too large, just a starter home, but I love it just the same."

"Well, I still live at home. In time, I'd like to move out, but I'm okay living there for now. I help my mom a lot with Colleen and Wyatt. Can you believe

Wyatt just turned twelve and Colleen's a junior in high school?"

"You're kidding me. I remember when she was a little thing! I can't believe Wyatt's twelve. I remember when he was born."

"Yep, I can't believe Colleen will be in college in one more year. I can still see her climbing on your bed in our old dorm room, playing hide and seek under the covers. Remember the curly mop of hair she had?"

Gabriella nodded.

"Now, it's straight as a pin," Angelina chuckled. "Oh, and can you believe she's already had universities contacting her to play field hockey for them? Time sure flies by, doesn't it?"

"It certainly does," Gabriella added in agreement. "What about Kelly and James? What are they up to?"

"Kelly is twenty-five now and is currently attending graduate school at Emory University, and James is twenty-seven. He's engaged to his high school sweetheart and has followed my dad into banking. How are your parents and brothers?"

Gabriella couldn't stop talking about her family as she helped Angelina finish hanging the remaining border on her bulletin boards. "Mom and Dad are semi-retired. As I'm sure you already know, Dad has turned over his medical practice to Alec and Joseph and works three days a week. He's kept his favorite patients, so I'm sure Colleen and Wyatt still see him. I'm not sure how much longer he'll practice since he has so many other interests. He worked so hard building that practice that I think he now believes he can successfully turn it over to my brothers.

"Alejandro just moved back to town. He lived in Madison, Wisconsin and worked for the University

Hospital. He's a renowned transplant surgeon and was recruited to head up the Transplant Services here. I think deep down he decided to come home because Mom and Dad are nearing retirement, and he wanted to spend more time with them as they get older. Being the oldest, he has a sense of responsibility to take care of them." Gabriella paused, twirling her hair as she thought about her brother. "I can't believe he's been gone since he left for college almost twenty years ago. He's thirty-seven now. Although, it came out of the blue, I think he's got other stuff going on and just wants to be near family."

"What do you think is going on with him? I remember how intense he was all the time when I talked with him on the phone, and then other times he was a jokester. Do you think he is running away from someone or something?"

Gabriella just looked at Angelina—she wasn't going to comment on what Angelina was saying.

Angelina continued, "I'm just glad that he's living in town now. Maybe I'll finally have a chance to meet him in person."

"Of course, you will. I'll make sure it happens." Thinking back, Gabriella said, "That's right. I forgot you've never met face to face. He was never around us... Was he?"

"No, he wasn't."

Gabriella stepped down from the ladder after completing the finishing touches on the bulletin board. She would make sure that would happen in the near future.

The school year started without issue two weeks before the Labor Day holiday. Angelina really enjoyed all of her students, and she was excited to be working with Gabriella. They both realized how much they'd truly missed their friendship. Graduating from college and entering the workforce was a hard transition, and they both realized they'd failed one another by not keeping their friendship alive. They started spending their weekends together shopping and going to their students' soccer games. They had a ball reliving their collegiate experiences and sharing their new life challenges.

The day after Labor Day, Angelina got a call out of the blue from Maria, Gabriella's mother. Gabriella was turning thirty the following week, September 9th, and her mother wanted to throw a surprise party for her only daughter. She wanted Angelina to put together a listing of the teachers at St. Margaret's. The party was scheduled for the first weekend of October, so Gabriella would be clueless as to the surprise.

Angelina was thrilled that Maria asked for her input, and she wasn't shy about volunteering to help Maria with the details. Angelina was crafty and immediately volunteered to make all of the party favors and invitations. Angelina designed the card that would be used as the invitation. Using her various supplies, she spent the entire weekend after Labor Day cutting paper, gluing flowers and addressing the large number of invitations that Maria needed. Maria was surprised with how quickly she completed everything in such a short amount of time.

Maria had thought of absolutely everything. She'd even arranged for Alejandro to spend the afternoon with Gabriella leading up to the party: Alejandro was going to take Gabriella to a matinée showing of Miss Saigon that was playing at the Opera House. Then, he was taking her to an early dinner. Of course, the early dinner would lead to her surprise party.

Alejandro picked Gabriella up for the musical the day of the party. She wouldn't stop talking about Angelina. She was elated that Angelina was working across the hall from her. "Alejandro, you've never actually met Angelina, have you?"

"I've heard a lot about her over the years since, what was it, your freshman year?"

"Yeah, we've known one another since our first semester of freshman year. Remember, at first we lived across the hall from one another?"

"That's right. I can't believe I've never met her in all these years."

"Well, now that we're working together, we'll have to go to happy hour so you two can meet. She's met everyone in the family except you. I think after all of these years you need to put the name and face together."

"I would have to agree. I talked to her often on the phone while you roomed together, but since I never had the chance to visit you, we never met. I'd love to put the name and the face together, but I don't know about happy hour. I'm sure we can meet at some point."

Gabriella thoroughly enjoyed the musical. As they walked out of the Opera House, Gabriella looped her arm through Alejandro's. "Thank you. This was such a treat. I've wanted to see that for a long time."

"I enjoyed it, too. Now, let's go have something to

eat."

"Alejandro."

"Yes?"

"Thank you."

"For what?"

"For today... For moving back home. I've missed you so much. I hardly saw you after you moved away to college. I know we've talked often but it wasn't the same... Now I feel like I have another brother again. I can see you whenever I want. I can relate to what you are doing and what you are experiencing. It's different, that's all. I love you so much."

Alejandro turned and pulled her into his arms. "I'm glad I came home, too. I missed seeing you grow up. You were only ten when I went away to school. I'd see you on holidays but that was it. I never got to experience your firsts with you. I should have been there for you, too, especially since you are the only girl in the family. We're going to remedy that now. I'm home to stay, and I expect to be as involved in your life as you want me to be. We need to plan regular outings because you mean way too much to me." Alejandro kissed her on the temple and said, "I love you, too."

Alejandro helped Gabriella into the car and pointed it towards the restaurant where the surprise party was scheduled for five o'clock. Conveniently, his phone rang as planned. He pulled off the highway to take the call. The call lasted a few minutes and they were on their way again.

"Was that the hospital?" He had talked to the person on the other end of the line cryptically so she wouldn't discover what they were discussing. He told a little white lie and said that he was speaking with his assistant who was following up on some travel arrangements.

Alejandro pulled into the parking lot of the restaurant and helped Gabriella from the car.

"I can't believe you brought me here. This is one of my favorite Italian restaurants."

"I'm glad I chose something you enjoy," he said as he opened the door to the restaurant.

As they entered the restaurant, the hostess asked if they would like to sit outdoors. They agreed since it was such a beautiful day. For a mid-autumn day, they were lucky with mild temperatures hovering in the mid-sixties. It was a welcome relief after the horribly hot and humid summer they'd had. "That's the one thing I've missed since moving back from Wisconsin. I forgot how awful the summers tend to be in St. Louis. Wisconsin is like this a good part of summer, nice and comfortable."

As the hostess led them to the patio, Alejandro winked at her. Gabriella smiled to herself thinking that only Alejandro would wink at the hostess. Unbeknownst to Gabriella, that was the hostess's cue to lead them to the backroom. She explained to Gabriella that this was an alternative route to their seating. The hostess threw open the doors and Gabriella was greeted with a loud, "Surprise!"

Gabriella was speechless as she threw her hands up to cover her mouth. She wasn't actually sure what was going on in front of her. As she walked further into the room, she noticed the streamers hanging from the ceiling and balloons scattered about the room. The partygoers all screamed, "Happy birthday!" in unison.

"What's this?" she asked Alejandro.

The room was packed with familiar faces when she noticed Angelina coming towards her from the back of the crowded room. She stopped in front of Gabriella, hugged her tightly, and said, "It's a surprise party for your birthday."

"But that was weeks ago," commented Gabriella. She turned to Alejandro and said, "You... You were you in on this, too?"

"Well..."

"Don't 'well' me—"

Alejandro grabbed her and gave her a big hug and kiss.

"Happy birthday, Sis. I'm so glad I could celebrate this milestone with you."

Gabriella greeted all of her guests. Her mother and Angelina moved into party mode, ensuring that everyone had everything they needed.

Instead of a sit down meal, Maria had arranged for a buffet to be served so that people could mingle and eat when they wanted to. The room was scattered with large, round tables covered in fall-colored tablecloths, with balloon bouquets being the focal point of each table. The yellow and orange colored balloons swayed in unison, highlighting the Mylar "Happy Birthday" balloons.

As everyone began to eat, Gabriella walked over to Angelina. She grabbed her arm and pulled her across the room where Alejandro was getting a drink. "I'd like you to finally meet someone." As Gabriella looped her arm through her brother's, she finally introduced her famous brother to her best friend. "Alejandro?"

"Yes?"

"I'd like you to finally meet my friend Angelina."

When he thought about it, he remembered seeing photos of her and Gabriella in school. He couldn't believe his eyes as he finally met her in person. Angelina was beautiful. She had honey colored eyes and long, light brown hair that had been neatly pulled back into a ponytail. Alejandro was stunned by their meeting and was pulled back into the moment.

Before Gabriella could say anymore, Alejandro was reaching for Angelina's hand. "Finally, we meet."

"Yes, finally. I've heard so much about you through the years." Angelina grasped his hand and was pulled into an embrace. She was taken aback by the gesture, but realized that she felt like she'd known him forever.

Before Angelina could get accustomed to the embrace, he was being waved down from across the room. "It was nice to finally meet you. We'll talk later."

Angelina smiled as he walked away. She was excited that she finally met Alejandro, but also wished they'd had more of a chance to visit in person.

Gabriella was disturbed that he left them so quickly. She gnawed on her lip in disbelief. It had taken her over twelve years for them to meet in person. In the blink of an eye, it was over. She wanted her best friend to finally get to know him since he was such an important part of her life.

Angelina knew Gabriella was upset with her brother. "Gabriella, don't think twice about our meeting. This is your party. Have fun! Alejandro and I can talk another time. You know he's just as popular as you, the birthday girl, since he's been away for so long."

Gabriella hugged her friend. "I know. I've just waited for this moment for so long," she said as she pulled away from Angelina.

Gabriella's party went well. The dancing began after dinner, and Alejandro cut in on their father while he was dancing with Gabriella. "Were you surprised?" he asked her.

"What do you think?"

"I'm glad you were. And I'm glad I was able to participate in this celebration."

"Alejandro?"

"Yes?"

"Will you do me a favor?"

"Sure, if I can."

"Angelina has been working tirelessly during this party. Will you at least dance with her? She needs a break." Gabriella was still upset with Alejandro for walking away from his initial meeting with Angelina. She knew her uncle had summoned him, but still. This was an important moment and she wanted her brother to get to know her best friend.

"Of course I will. I am glad that you were able to reconnect with each other. I know she was an important part of your collegiate days. What happened for you to lose touch with one another?"

"I'm really not sure. I guess we became so involved in our new lives. With our first teaching jobs, we were extremely busy that first summer. Getting things together for the classroom, writing lesson plans, coming up with innovative ideas... I remember going into the classroom almost every day that summer after I got my first job. Planning, always planning. I wanted to be the best teacher that I could be, someone my students would always remember. I hope I've done that through the years. Angelina was going about it the same way. I remember we always had the same ambitions. We wanted to be the best..."

"Well, from what you've told me through the years, you've been an influence on many students. I am so proud of you."

"As I am of you. Now, go and have that dance with

my best friend." Alejandro brushed a kiss across her knuckles and headed towards Angelina.

"May I have this dance?"

"Alejandro, I'd love to but I am busy at the moment. How about later?"

Alejandro reached for her hand, but she pulled it away.

He had a funny look on his face—one of surprise that she wouldn't dance with him. He knew Gabriella had been upset with him earlier when he'd been summoned by their uncle. He wanted to spend some time with Angelina, but he knew his uncle would have made a scene, so he'd left her standing with his sister.

The look Gabriella had sent his way when he walked away was the same one she used to give him when she was a little girl and he wouldn't give into her demands. She'd scrunch her face and roll her eyes at him. He knew he was in trouble with his sister, and he needed to make up to her by dancing with Angelina.

"Aww, come on."

"Give me a few minutes to finish this up, and I'll dance with you."

While Angelina was cleaning up, Alejandro got an emergency call. He had to rush to the hospital to tend to a patient who'd had a kidney transplant and was exhibiting signs of infection. Alejandro hated getting these calls. He apologized to Gabriella for having to leave early. She understood but thought he needed to have some fun in his life.

She was going to see that he did, now that he was home and living close by.

Chapter Two

THE FOLLOWING MONDAY MORNING, GABRIELLA couldn't wait to see Angelina. She ran directly into Angelina's classroom, hugged, and thanked her for helping her mother organize and plan her surprise party. "I had such a wonderful time."

"I did, too. It was great seeing everyone. I was happy to finally meet Alejandro in person. Were you surprised?"

"Surprised? Yes, that's an understatement. Shocked is more like it. I wasn't sure what was happening at first, but then you came running up to me. All I can say is Alejandro did a fabulous job of keeping it from me. I thought it was his idea to take me to Miss Saigon."

"It was his idea. We weren't sure how to get you there, so he volunteered. It was really important to him that he take you to the play since you wanted to see it so badly. He wanted to make it a special memory for you since he missed so many important happenings in your life. He was like a kid in a candy store helping your mother plan this part of the surprise. He even met with the hostess at the restaurant so she knew who he was and could guide you directly to the party without question."

"Huh, so that's what that wink was about."

"What wink?"

"Never mind. Getting back to Alejandro… I thought you hadn't met before the party."

"We hadn't. Your mother arranged it all. I didn't meet him until you introduced us."

"Oh. Did you two have a good time dancing?"

"We never danced. I told him I was busy. I was getting the party favors together because one of your mom's friends was leaving, and I wanted to be sure she had one. I asked if he could wait a few minutes, and when I went looking for him, he was gone."

"Oh, I'm sorry. I thought you'd danced. He got a call from the hospital and had to go in."

"After all of these years, I was just glad to finally meet him in the flesh. I'd talked to him while we were in school, and I've met Alec and Joe many times. It's just nice after all of these years to finally meet him in person. I always enjoyed talking with him. He always knew the right thing to say to brighten my day."

Mid-October was upon them, and with it came Colleen's field hockey sectionals. Colleen, Angelina's sister, played for her high school team. She was the star of the team and a team player who always thought of her teammates first while on the field. She'd broken many of her high school's prestigious records. She was only a junior, but had already received letters from various universities that were interested in her playing field hockey for them.

The team had a game scheduled in Kansas City, which was a four hour drive from St. Louis. Colleen's parents and brother, Wyatt (who always attended her matches), were going to follow the bus to Kansas City. Wyatt loved watching his older sister play. He played ice hockey himself and was a well-respected player in his own right.

Angelina declined to take the early morning car ride to Kansas City with her parents. She was preparing for the end of the first quarter and wanted to spend the weekend working on grades. She never liked waiting until the last minute to complete the quarterly report card.

They were originally scheduled to leave directly after school ended on Friday afternoon, but at the last minute the plans were changed. The new plan was to leave at seven o'clock Saturday morning.

Angelina spent Friday evening at Gabriella's house. It was the first time Angelina had been to Gabriella's. As soon as she pulled up to the curb, she fell in love with it. The sidewalk was lined with flowers. She remembered how much Gabriella loved flowers—she had always been buying bouquets of whatever flowers she could get her hands on for their dorm room.

Gabriella had told Angelina that her home was a starter house and Angelina couldn't believe the size of it. The house fit the neighborhood. It was a typical red brick two-story with an attached garage. Angelina couldn't wait to see the inside as the outside was so Gabriella, between the size, red brick and swing that sat on the front porch.

She rang the doorbell and Gabriella answered instan-taneously—she had been waiting for Angelina right by the door. She gave Angelina a quick tour of her four-bedroom home. It had a gourmet kitchen that any chef would envy, as well as a formal dining room that held a table she was sure would fit at least eight, and maybe even twelve when opened fully. She had a quaint living room that fit the house, and a huge family room that overlooked a fairly large backyard. The backyard was strewn with flowers blooming in pots and baskets of flowers hanging from a multitude of shepherd's hooks. Fall was in the air and, thankfully, St. Louis hadn't experienced a frost yet, so Angelina could fully enjoy Gabriella's brightly colored backyard and patio area.

Gabriella had ordered pizza. As they waited for the deliveryman, Angelina commented on her home. "I thought you said this was a starter home."

"It is."

"If this is what you consider a starter home, I can only imagine what your next house will look like."

"It's not that big, Angelina. I've done a few updates over the years. You should have seen it when I first bought it."

"All I can say is this house is so you, inside and out— between the flowers, the red brick… and I love how you decorated it." She barely finished her comment when the doorbell rang. They'd decided to eat in as Gabriella wanted Angelina to experience pizza from the neighborhood pizzeria. "Doesn't this remind you of our late-night pizza parties that we held in our dorm room?" asked Angelina.

"Yeah, but now we can at least enjoy our food without being interrupted by the guys from the other side of the dorm. I swear they had a homing device when a pizza crossed through the elevators doors."

"I know. They were crazy."

They finished their meal, and then Angelina helped Gabriella prepare the pictures that would hang on her bulletin board dedicated to the special events from the quarter. They learned the importance of this in one of their education classes. It helped with parent teacher conferences, as the bulletin board tied up the quarter, highlighting the field trips, parties, and whatever else occurred that was special. It was a fabulous way for parents who couldn't attend the special functions to see what occurred in their children's lives. Angelina had put the finishing touches on her display while they waited for their pizza.

During their evening, many topics were discussed. Angelina started talking about the special events they attended while in college. "Gabriella, do you remember when we had to go on that urban experience for one of our education classes, were dropped off in the middle of the city with hardly a map, and were expected to visit the city schools and find our way downtown?"

"Yeah, I do. I really enjoyed seeing all of the old, turn-of-the-century schools. The architecture was beautiful. I wish the buildings would have been maintained more." Pausing, Gabriella added, "I can understand how the buildings fell into the condition they're in. Some, in fact many, of them have since closed. Some of those neighborhoods were pretty scary."

They continued their reminiscing and hardly noticed that three hours had elapsed when the doorbell rang. "Are you expecting anyone?" asked Angelina as Gabriella stood to open the door.

"At this hour? No. I'd intended it to be just a girl's

night."

Before she could get to the door, the bell rang again. "Wait a minute… Just wait a minute… Who is it, anyway?" called Gabriella. She turned to Angelina and whispered, "One should always ask before opening the door especially at this late hour."

"Me," a voice called from the other side of the door.

"Who's me?"

"You know who it is. Open the door, Gabriella."

Gabriella threw open the door and was pulled into a hug. "Alejandro, what're you doing here?"

"Saying hello to my favorite sister."

"Favorite? You mean only."

"Okay, okay. Enough of that."

Gabriella led Alejandro to the family room where they'd been working.

"What're you doing this evening?" asked Alejandro as Gabriella led him down the hallway.

"Angelina and I are working on our quarterly bulletin boards. We take pictures throughout the year and post them in our classroom at the end of the quarter. That way the students and parents can experience some of the fun activities we did throughout the quarter."

"Sounds like a good idea," he said as he moved into the room. "Hi, Angelina. How are you doing?"

"I'm fine," Angelina smiled at Alejandro. "And you?"

"I'm great!" Alejandro said with a grin. "I'm off service with the hospital for the week and can finally take it easy. Thankfully, I just have office hours. These last few weeks since Gabriella's party have been a blur— I've worked non-stop. I'm so looking forward to some down time."

"Want something to drink?" Gabriella asked as she

turned towards the kitchen.

"Sure, whatever you have," he called out as she disappeared around the corner.

Alejandro stood looking at Angelina as she put the finishing touches on Gabriella's bulletin board. "So, are you the creative genius behind this project? I heard you made the invitations for Gabriella's party. They were beautiful."

Angelina put down the last of the pictures. Smiling, she looked over her shoulder at him. As she flashed her smile, she chuckled and said, "No, I'm not the genius. Your sister did much of this herself... And thank you for your compliment. I had a lot of fun helping your mother."

"From what I hear, you more than helped. I know my mom really appreciated everything you did to make it a special day for my sister."

Gabriella returned with a glass of wine. They sat around the table, catching up.

"I'm sorry I didn't get a chance to have that dance with you, Angelina."

"It's not a problem. I understand. I was trying to get the party favors together for one of your mom's friends and, when I went looking for you, you were already gone. Gabriella explained that you were called into the hospital. We can have that dance anytime."

Alejandro truly loved his sister and Angelina saw it first-hand. She had no idea that he'd missed Gabriella as much as he had while he'd lived out of state. Alejandro was a kind, caring man who seemed to really enjoy his job. Even with the demands of his profession, he spoke highly of his peers and co-workers at the hospital. He was unlike any doctor that she knew. He was compassionate and didn't talk down as he spoke of his colleagues.

Angelina saw a much different side to him than she imagined when she looked back on her many conversations they'd had while she was in college. She saw the serious side to him, but also the jokester that loved to kid around. But now he was different. He seemed much more intent—serious, but he was still a loving brother.

She caught him staring at her a few times and, several times, she smiled back at him, causing him to look away.

They talked until two in the morning when Angelina finally decided to go home. She explained that the following morning she wanted to be sure and be up to wish Colleen good luck before she left for her tournament. Angelina said her good-byes while Alejandro decided to stay with Gabriella. "It's been a long time since we've done this."

"It has. So how come you came by tonight?"

"I hadn't seen you since your party and wanted to spend some time with you."

Gabriella decided to change the subject abruptly, "I've got a question for you." She'd noticed him staring at Angelina several times while they talked.

"And that is?"

"Are you seeing anyone?"

"No," he sternly replied.

"Why not?" she asked.

"I'm too busy getting acclimated to my new job."

"Come on now…"

"Not now, Gabby. I don't want to talk about it." She knew he meant business—he usually only called her Gabby when he was upset with her. She dropped her questioning for the time being. She had her hopes, but she wasn't going to share them with Alejandro.

Angelina had barely crawled into bed when her alarm blared in her ear. It was six in the morning and she felt like she'd just gone to sleep. She crawled out of bed and dressed quickly, as she wanted to see her parents off.

Angelina hugged Colleen and wished her good luck as she and her parents hurried out the door. Colleen had to be at school by seven to make the bus for their early afternoon game. "Drive safely," she told her parents as she kissed them goodbye. "Wyatt, be sure and catch the entire game on video."

"I will," he told her as he grabbed a bagel and ran out the door. "Don't forget to walk Bingo," he yelled as he closed the car door. Bingo was the family's shelter dog they'd adopted. They'd had him for the last six years. He was a mix breed that the whole family had fallen in love with when they first laid eyes on him. Within hours of him entering their house, he'd become a member of the family. He was a sweet dog who let strangers know of his presence. They didn't think he'd bite anyone, but they didn't want to test him either.

Angelina went back to bed for a few hours, then spent the day as planned. She finished grading the last of the tests that she would use for the quarter. She was pleased with her students' grades. All of them had done well. That would bode well for her, especially since this was her first quarter at St. Margaret's. Angelina took pride in her job and loved to see her students doing well.

Angelina decided to take a break and headed to the nearest local bookstore. Her favorite mystery author had just released a new book and she wanted to start it that weekend as a reward for finishing her grades for the quarter. She also wanted to read something new, in addition to the mystery that she held in her hand. She wasn't sure what she was looking for, and was searching the endcaps for new releases when she turned and accidentally bumped into someone, causing herself to drop her book. She looked up and was surprised to see Alejandro. "What're you doing here?" she asked as she knelt down to pick up the book from the floor.

"I could ask you the same," he said as he also reached for her book. "Sorry about that. I didn't mean to scare you into dropping your book."

"You didn't scare me."

"Well, I'm glad." he said, laughing. "If you're not in a hurry to be somewhere, would you be interested in having a coffee?"

Smiling at him, she teased, "I guess if you twisted my arm I could have one."

Smiling broadly at her, he paused and said, "Okay, I'm twisting," and he reached for her arm and playfully twisted it. Laughing, they headed towards the café.

The barista took their order and Alejandro graciously paid for their coffees. Angelina ordered a café mocha, while Alejandro chose a plain old cup of coffee.

"You're not too adventurous."

"What do you mean?"

"Plain coffee?"

"What can I say?" he chuckled as he led her to a table in the back of the café. They sat and talked. "Angelina, I am so glad that you and Gabriella were able to reconnect. I think she considers you a sister. She has Alec,

Joe, and I, but brothers are brothers. You can't talk 'girl' talk with us."

"I consider her a sister as well. I can share things with her that I can't share with my own sister, Kelly. I guess it's because we're the same age. Gabriella's a special person. I am lucky to have her in my life."

"I know she feels that same about you." Alejandro took a sip of his coffee, "So, what're your plans for the day?"

"Well, I worked on grades earlier. I got up early since my parents, Colleen, and Wyatt were heading off to Kansas City for Colleen's field hockey game. I thought I'd take a break, and that's how I ended up here. I'm not sure how I am going to spend the rest of the weekend. I guess take it easy." Pointing to her book, she added, "And read."

"Since you have no real plans outside of reading, what about having dinner with me?"

"Alejandro, that's kind of you to ask." She was surprised with his invitation and she paused before responding, smiling broadly. She said, "Sure, I'll have dinner with you." She knew his sister would be thrilled just as she was. She had always enjoyed her phone conversations with him, but now she was able to see him in a different light. When he talked, she could see the intensity on his face and witness the passion in his eyes when he discussed something close to his heart. She was excited, to say the least, to have dinner with him—she was seeing a much different side to his personality than she'd imagined coming through the phone.

They finished their drinks and he said, "Why don't I follow you home and then we can decide where to go."

"Sounds great."

"Ready?" Angelina nodded and Alejandro stood and helped her with her chair. She paid for two books: the mystery she'd originally sought out and a non-fiction book written by one of her favorite comedians. Alejandro escorted her to her car and asked that she wait while he retrieved his car.

Angelina waited in her car for Alejandro. She sat there replaying their conversation. She hadn't paid much attention to his looks at Gabriella's party and when she saw him at Gabriella's house, it was late, and she was tired after a long day of teaching. But today… today she saw him for the man he was. *Wow*, she thought. "How did I miss how attractive he is?" she said aloud to herself. He'd certainly matured into quite a man from what she remembered from his pictures. She was sure a passersby thought she was crazy talking to herself sitting alone in her car. But, she had to talk to someone, and that someone was herself.

My gosh! He's practically beautiful, she screamed in her head. *He has the most amazing dark eyes.* His Spanish ancestry only added to his looks with his dark skin tone. His hair was also dark and thick, cut short and made for running one's fingers through. She had to get ahold of herself. She shouldn't be thinking of Gabriella's brother in these terms. *Anyway, he wouldn't look twice at me,* she thought. *But wait a minute… he did at Gabriella's house. No, I'm sure I imagined that… And that smile. Stop, just stop it—I'm not going there. Just friends. That's right, we're just friends.*

She couldn't believe how quickly her plans had changed and, with that, she heard a short toot signifying that he was ready. She waved at him, acknowledging his presence and put her car into reverse. As she took her foot off the brake, her heart rate accelerated as she backed out of her parking space. She stopped to turn and put her car into drive. *Stop it,* she said to herself. *I'm not nervous. This is Alejandro. We're friends. There's no need to be nervous,* she thought as she drove off towards home, Alejandro following closely behind.

In her fifteen minute drive home, she convinced herself not to be nervous. This was just dinner with a friend, that's all.

She pulled into her driveway with Alejandro right behind her. Her purse toppled over when she made the sharp turn into her driveway, but she quickly grabbed the contents of her purse and motioned to Alejandro that she needed to run into the house—she didn't realize that her cell phone was lodged between the seats.

Alejandro made a quick call while he waited for her. She ran inside, quickly let Bingo out, and grabbed a jacket since it was expected to be a cool evening. She locked the house and walked over to Alejandro's car. He got out of his car and held the door open for her, even assisting her with her seat belt.

"Where would you like to go?" he asked.

"I don't care. You choose."

"Why don't we head towards Old Towne, walk around, and when we're ready we'll just pick a spot to eat."

"Sounds like a plan."

They drove for a few miles before Angelina asked Alejandro what he liked to do in his spare time. Even though she tried not to be nervous, she was. She didn't understand what was wrong with her. It's not like this was a blind date.

"I like the outdoors. I'd be outside all of the time if

I could. I used to run around the lakes up in Madison, but I wasn't able to do that much before I moved home. I love going to Forest Park, but I don't get there very often due to my schedule at the hospital and the distance from my house. I wish it were right around the corner, but it isn't. I'm surrounded by farmland now: corn and cows."

"You should try and make time for yourself... I know that's hard with your schedule and all. Do you anticipate it improving?"

"I hope so. I'm still trying to get the lay of the hospital. I'm glad that I made the move, but there's always an adjustment when you change jobs."

"I know that too well. When St. Mark's closed, I was pretty lost, especially since we went right into summer. I'm just thankful that I still live at home. I was able to help my mom with my siblings. My dad's been pretty busy at the bank, so I did the majority of the yard work. I love my family and would do absolutely anything for them."

"They're lucky to have you. Have you ever wanted to get out on your own?"

"Yes and no. I'm pretty independent, and my parents don't stop me from doing anything. I pay them rent, although I know they're putting it away for me for when I do decide to move out. My parents are great."

Alejandro parked and came around to help Angelina from the car. *He's a true gentleman,* she thought. Opening car doors, holding doors for her... She almost thought that was a lost trait of many men. Most of the men she dated let her open her own doors, never helped her from the car, and often proceeded her going through doors before her. She often wondered if all men had lost their manners. She was pleasantly surprised that Alejandro was so unlike her previous boyfriends. And she liked it—she liked having doors held open for her, liked being made to feel special.

Side by side, they walked the streets of Old Towne, looking into the windows of the closed stores. Alejandro didn't seem to mind that Angelina liked to go into the antique stores. "I have a fondness for antiques as well," he told her as they exited the final store on the block. "Hungry, yet?"

"I'm a little hungry. What time is it?"

"Just about seven."

"I guess Colleen's game should be about over. Wyatt was going to videotape it for me. Depending on my schedule, I usually try to get to as many games as I can. Today, I just didn't feel like taking the trip. I wanted to get my grades done, and I guess just vegetate a little this weekend." They stopped at a restaurant and looked at the menu displayed in the window. Neither liked what was on the menu and walked on.

"From the time I accepted my job at St. Margaret's, it's been a whirlwind with trying to get ready for the school year. I had less than a week to prepare my classroom and get ready. I was a little lost at first as I changed grades and had to start all over on my lesson plans. I pretty much like to have the whole year planned out, and I spent all of my weekends since I took the job planning that."

They walked down the sidewalk. A bunch of kids came running towards her. Alejandro put his arm around her to keep her from being knocked into. She smiled up at him and continued with the conversation.

"Gabriella helped me so much. I couldn't have done it without her. This is the first weekend that I felt I needed to take time for myself. And then I see you at the bookstore. This has been a great day. Thank you for this evening. I'm really enjoying myself."

"I'm glad. I'm having a good time getting to know you, too."

They had dinner at a pub on Main Street. It was nothing fancy, but they sat and took in the ambience. They both enjoyed a beer while they waited for their food to arrive. Angelina had ordered a plate of nachos while Alejandro ordered a BLT. "I haven't had a BLT in years," he said. "This last time was—"

He stopped midsentence and didn't finish his thought. She noticed him tense up and a look of sadness crossed his face. He looked down at his left hand like he was looking for something, paused, and then changed the subject. She felt uncomfortable for a moment, but then when he started talking again, the feeling passed.

When they had finished their dinner and were having a coffee, the weekend band started playing. The band played a mix of country, pop, and seventies/eighties music. Several couples started to dance. Alejandro glanced at Angelina, reached out his hand and said, "Shall we dance?"

Angelina nodded and stood. The band had started the opening melody to a famous ballad as they made their way across the dance floor. Alejandro escorted her to the middle of the floor where he gently pulled her into his arms. He sensed her nervousness, but didn't question it. No words were spoken. They felt each beat to the music and danced. They glided across the dance floor until the music ended. He brushed a kiss across her knuckles, thanking her for the dance. Alejandro placed his hand on her lower back, guiding her back to their table. The instant she felt his hand on her back, she jumped and her nerves returned once again. She didn't understand what was wrong with her. That small gesture shouldn't have affected her in the manner it did.

Alejandro felt her jump when he guided her back to their table. He wasn't sure what had caused her nervousness, but he decided to call it a night. "It's getting late. Shall we go?"

He paid the bill. As they exited the restaurant, he placed his arm around her shoulders and guided her from the restaurant. The nervousness he had felt earlier when they left the dance floor had disappeared. They silently walked to Alejandro's car. He was helping her into her seat when he realized that he'd turned off his cell phone while they were at dinner. As he headed around the back of the car, he turned it on and discovered that he'd missed three phone calls, all from his father.

Since it was nearing midnight, he decided not to return his father's calls. He'd never left a message, so Alejandro didn't think it was anything too important. Alejandro drove Angelina home and walked her to the door.

"I had a really nice time this evening," she said.

"So did I. We'll have to do this again sometime soon… I know my schedule's pretty busy starting next week. Maybe we can get together and have dinner again when my schedule clears." He whipped out his cell phone. "Give me your number and I'll call you when I have some free time."

She gave him her number then he walked her to her door. Angelina unlocked the door and turned back to Alejandro. He thanked her again, turned, and left her standing in the doorway.

Angelina waved goodbye as he walked away. Reflecting on her day, she realized what a remarkable man Alejandro was. She knew she'd liked him from the phone conversations they'd had and from what Gabriella had told her over the years, but she hadn't realized what a kind person he really was. The way he spoke of his family, friends, and colleagues spoke volumes about the person he was.

It was nearing one in the morning when Alejandro pulled into his driveway. As he opened his door, his cell rang. He looked at the caller ID and saw that it was his father. "Hey, Dad. I saw that you'd called earlier but was out and thought it was too late to return your call. What's up?"

"Where are you?"

"I just got home. I'm sitting in my driveway."

"Can you do me a favor?"

"Sure. What ya need?"

"Will you go over to Gabriella's for me? Pick her up and take her over to Angelina's."

"Why? What's wrong?"

"Gabriella's been trying to get a hold of her. She wasn't answering her cell."

"Is there a problem?"

"Alejandro, Colleen was in a serious accident."

"What happened?"

"I don't know all of the details. I just know she's in the ICU at Kansas City Memorial. She was injured in her field hockey game. Her parents have tried unsuccessfully to get ahold of Angelina. They called me since I'm her physician, and I told them I'd have Gabriella go over and break the news to her."

"What can I do?"

"Just get over to Gabriella's ASAP. When you get to Angelina's, call me and hopefully I'll have some more information." Alejandro hung up the phone, closed the car door, revved up his engine, and headed straight for Gabriella's. Before he could ring the bell, the door flew open and she was running out the door.

"Hurry, we've got to get to Angelina's!"

The lights were still on at Angelina's when they pulled up. It had barely been forty-five minutes since he left her on the doorstep. They ran to the door and rang the bell. Angelina looked out the front window prior to opening the door. "Alejandro, Gabriella, why're you here? Is something wrong?"

Alejandro had dialed his father as they approached the house. The call had just connected when Angelina opened the door. "Gabriella?" she asked again as she looked at her friend.

Alejandro told his father they were at Angelina's, and he asked to speak with her. Angelina looked scared. "What's wrong? Did something happen to my parents?"

Alejandro passed the phone to her. "My father would like to speak with you."

They entered the foyer and Alejandro closed the door behind them.

"Dr. A? What's wrong?" Angelina asked.

Alejandro led her to the couch and gestured for her to sit. Gabriella and Alejandro flanked her on either side.

"Angelina, are you sitting?"

"Yes, I am. What's wrong?"

"Angelina, Colleen's been in an accident. She was seriously injured in her field hockey game and is in the ICU."

Angelina raised a shaking hand to her mouth in shock.

"What happened?" she asked, trying to hold back her emotions.

"I'm not sure. I just know she took a shot to the abdomen from a very close range and collapsed onto the field. Your parents rushed to her, but by the time they got to her, she was unconscious. They rushed her to the hospital and called me since I am her physician, but also because of your relationship with Gabriella."

Gabriella grabbed Angelina's hand, and Alejandro put his arm around her.

"I need to go there and be with my sister."

"Angelina, I'm not sure that is a good idea. Do you have a piece of paper handy?"

Alejandro heard his father's request and pulled a notepad from his pocket. He always carried a notebook with him in the event he received an emergency call. "Here," he said.

Angelina was shaking so badly that she handed the phone to Alejandro. He wrote the telephone number down for the hospital, along with the name of the doctor that was handling Colleen's case. Angelina just sat mumbling, "I should have been there…"

Alejandro disconnected the call and turned to Angelina. "What can I do?" he asked.

"I don't know," she stammered. "I need to talk to my parents. I wonder if Kelly and James know."

While Gabriella got Angelina a glass of water, Alejandro called the hospital. He was able to get through to the nurses' station and speak with the nurse in charge. "Hello, yes, my name is Dr. Alejandro Alvarez. I am a friend of Colleen Samuels's sister. She is sitting right here with me. What is her condition?"

The nurse didn't want to divulge anything in relation to her condition since she couldn't verify who they were. "Fine," he said. "Are her parents nearby so that we can talk to them?"

The nurse placed them on hold while she went to get Angelina's mother. Angelina's mother came on the phone. "Hello," she stuttered.

"Mrs. Samuels?"

"Yes."

"This is Alejandro, Dr. A.'s son. I am here with Angelina. I'll put her on." Alejandro handed the phone to Angelina.

"Angelina?"

"Mom… Colleen… What happened? What's wrong with her?"

"Sweetie, she somehow took a hard shot directly in the abdomen. She cried out and collapsed. By the time we reached her, she was unconscious. She has significant swelling in the abdomen and they're waiting on the CT scan. She was having difficulties breathing, so they decided to put her into ICU until they can determine what's wrong with her."

"Mom, I'll be there as soon as I can."

"Honey, no wait. Let's see what the test results reveal. I'm in contact with Alejandro's father and we'll go from there. Where is your cell phone? I tried calling several times—there was no answer."

"I don't know. I had it earlier in the day." Angelina thought for a moment and then realized that it probably had fallen out of her purse when it overturned in her car. "It must have fallen out of my purse. I think it's in my car."

"Okay. Now try not to worry. I'll call you as soon as we know something. Is Gabriella with you?"

"Yes, she is."

"Good. I don't want you alone. Is Alejandro still with you?"

"Yes."

"Let me speak with him."

She handed the phone to Alejandro.

"Hello?"

"Alejandro?"

"Yes."

"I want to thank you and Gabriella for being there with Angelina. I told Angelina that I want her to stay there until we know something. The doctors are in contact with your father. I'm not sure what's going to happen, but we may have Colleen flown back to St. Louis. We have to see how she gets through the night. I would appreciate it if you could stay with Angelina as long as you can."

"It's not a problem."

"Please watch over her. I'm sure she has some guilt since she wasn't here. I'll call with any updates."

"Thanks." Alejandro disconnected the call and turned to Angelina. "Your mom will call with any updates. Why don't you try and get some rest?"

"I can't. My sister's in the hospital in serious condition. I want to be with her."

"I realize that, but the best place for you is right here. Let's not overreact. We need to wait for a more complete diagnosis."

Angelina got up and ran to her car where she discovered her cell phone lodged between the seats. Gabriella decided to make coffee when Angelina returned from her car with her phone in hand. Alejandro sat with Angelina while she paced the room. "What could be wrong with her?"

"I can't say for sure until the test results come back. It may be nothing."

The three of them stayed-up the remainder of the night. There was little talking. Gabriella held Angelina's hand while Alejandro sat, staring off into space. He was racking his brain with her possible diagnosis.

Just before dawn, Angelina drifted off to sleep. Earlier, Gabriella had curled up into an armchair and had also fallen asleep. Alejandro had joined Angelina on the couch. She'd fallen asleep in his arms.

I HOPE YOU ENJOYED READING THE first two chapters of Life's Second Chances. It is currently available for purchase. Please visit my website www. Annestoneauthor.com for further information.

Author's Note

THANK YOU SO MUCH FOR reading Life's Forever Changed, the Prequel to The Show Me Series. If you would like to be notified about new releases, please sign up for my newsletter. You'll be treated to sneak peeks, giveaways, free books and bonus material just for signing up.

If you enjoyed reading Life's Forever Changed, please consider leaving a review.

Reviews are always appreciated!

Anne

About the Author

ANNE STONE WAS BORN AND raised in St. Louis, MissAnne Stone was born and raised in St. Louis, Missouri but now lives in the cold state of Wisconsin with her faithful Cavalier King Charles Spaniel. She writes heartfelt sweet contemporary romance and is the author of the Show Me and Williams & Company series. She loves to tell a story and that's what you'll definitely get in an Anne Stone novel.

Anne's degree is in education but she has worked in the corporate sector managing a large number of staff. Now, she works from home where part of her day is still spent in the corporate world and the other part is dreaming of her heroes and heroines.

Anne loves to share giveaways and free books through her newsletters. Sign-up to learn more about her new releases.

Learn more about Anne by visiting www.AnneStoneAuthor.com.

Connect with Anne online:
Visit Anne's website: Annestoneauthor.com
Follow Anne on Facebook at: Anne Stone Author
Follow Anne on Twitter at: @AuthorAnneStone
Email Anne at: Anne@Annestoneauthor.com

Also by Anne Stone

The Show Me Series:
Life's Second Chances
Life's Gateway to Happiness
Life's Turned Upside Down
Life's Second Journey (Coming soon)
The Show Me Series Boxed Set: Vol 1 (Books 1-3)

Williams & Company:
Never Lose Hope